# SPOOK HOLLOW

TALES OF OZARK HORROR

# SPOOK HOLLOW

## TALES OF OZARK HORROR

### VOLUME ONE

EDITED BY HEATHER DAUGHRITY

Parlor Ghost Press

*Published by Parlor Ghost Press, an imprint of
Watertower Hill Publishing, LLC
Copyright © 2026 by Parlor Ghost Press
www.watertowerhill.com
www.parlorghostpress.com*

*Cover design by Christy Aldridge at Grim Poppy Design
Cover creation by Susan Roddey
at The Snark Shop by Phoenix & Fae Creations
Cover copyright © 2026, Parlor Ghost Press
Interior format by Joshua Daughrity at Watertower Hill Publishing, LLC*

*All rights reserved. No part of this book may be reproduced in any form without prior written permission of the author and publisher—other than for "fair use" as brief quotations embodied in articles and reviews.*

*Publisher's Note:
All characters and names in this book are fictional and are not designed, patterned after, nor descriptive of any person, living or deceased, except those used with permission.
Any similarities to people, living or deceased is purely by coincidence, except those used for historical fiction use.
Author and Publisher are not liable for any other likeness described herein.*

Library of Congress Cataloging-in-Publication Data has been applied for. (2/4/26)

*Trade Paperback ISBN: 978-1-965546-26-0
ASIN: B0GMY9R4GB*

Printed in the United States of America
First Edition
10 9 8 7 6 5 4 3 2 1

# TABLE OF CONTENTS

INTRODUCTION – Heather Daughrity ........................................................ i
GRANNYWOMAN LIZ – Teel James Glenn .............................................. 1
THREE STEPS PAST THE ELM – Fendy S. Tulodo ................................ 19
NSFW – Xavier Poe Kane ........................................................................... 39
WHO GOES WHERE? – Andrew Kurtz ..................................................... 49
SONGBIRD LANE – Troy Seate ................................................................. 63
SPEAK, THAT THE FLAME MAY SLEEP – Zary Fekete ..................... 75
BUILD TO SUIT – Amanda DeBord ........................................................... 89
UNDERFOOT OF THE GOWROW – D.R. Cook ................................... 105
THE SPRING – Zack Graham .................................................................... 127
THE APPLE AND THE TREE – Richard Beauchamp ........................... 145
DADDY – Ann Wuehler ............................................................................. 163
THE HOLLOW BELOW – Bella Chacha ................................................. 175
THE SERPENT OF EDEN – D. Winchester ............................................ 189
ABOUT THE AUTHORS ..........................................................................

# INTRODUCTION
## HEATHER DAUGHRITY

The Ozarks.
    The word itself has a shape of its own, the sound of it something beautiful yet dangerous, a comfort and a mystery. The beginning 'O' speaks of roundness, fullness, a coming-home, if you will. This is followed by that sharpest letter, 'Z,' which punctures the lovely daylight bubble of the 'O' and runs sharp along the tongue with premonitions of breathless nights in moonless valleys. The rest of the word—'arks'— brings a picture of arching mountaintops, but also of darkness.
    The Ozarks are a land of contradiction and enigma.

By day, calm, rolling hills and soaring trees provide a landscape of peace and calm.

> *We are in the Ozarks at last, just in the beginning of them, and they are beautiful. We passed along the foot of some hills and could look up their sides. The trees and rocks are lovely. Manly says we could almost live on the looks of them. ... The road goes uphill and down, and it is rutted and dusty and stony but every turn of the wheels changes our view of the woods and the hills. The sky seems lower here, and it is the softest blue. The distances and the valleys are blue whenever you can see them. It is a drowsy country that makes you feel wide awake and alive but somehow contented.*
> -Laura Ingalls Wilder, On the Way Home

But by night another feeling altogether pervades the air, one of secrets and old, old magic.

The Ozarks, which stretch over northern Arkansas and southern Missouri, with rocky foothills extending west into Oklahoma and a small part of Kansas, are millennia old, with speculation that they and the Appalachians to the east may have originally come from the same land mass, a mass that broke apart in that time of the world's history when whole continents were moving and settling into the places we modern folk now recognize.

Those more accustomed to the sharp, pointed peaks of the Rockies may find the Ozarks underwhelming; the Ozarks are thought to be ten times as old as their cousins to the west, and Time has wrought his vengeance on them.

> *Someone visiting the Ozarks ... will inevitably say, "What mountains?" For they're the oldest and have been worn away till mere nubs of their former selves poke out of the encompassing eroded limestone, barely match to be known as hills.*
> *-Marideth Sisco, singer and storyteller, in a performance given at the 2023 Smithsonian Folklife Festival*

But the Ozarks have a majesty all their own. Theirs is a subtle beauty, a deceptively gentle strength.

They have a mystery, too. A magic.

Once the fog rolls in.

> *"There is no romance if there is no fog. When everything is clear, there's no element of mystery. In the Ozarks, mystique is ubiquitous."*
> *-Jarod Kintz, The Lewis and Clark of the Ozarks*

I grew up in northeastern Oklahoma, in an area known as the "foothills of the Ozarks." Day trips or weekends into the mountains were common, and always, always, as we drove east toward the mountain peaks in the far distance, was the fog.

Rising up from dew-fresh fields and sitting low in countless valleys, a shroud of spectral mist in the darker places and a glimmer of gold in the air in those areas already kissed by the sun, the Ozark mist lingers just long enough to make her presence felt, a thrill in the bones that is part peaceful appreciation and part anxious wonder.

The Ozarks are a patchwork of rock and tree, stream and lake, cave and holler. The mountains themselves are riddled in places with tunnels and subterranean caverns. The forests stretch on, seemingly endless. The streams burble happily while the lakes rest placidly, cold and deep. And the hollers...

Oh, those Ozark hollers and their multitude of tales.

A colorful history and folklore tradition is sure to abound in a region filled with places with names like Lick Skillet, Pumpkin Center, Possum

Trot, Chicken Bustle, Booger Hollow, Jerktail, Knob Noster, Cooter, and Peculiar. The Ozarks are full of tales of boogers, haints, and hags, stories of grannywomen and their backwoods magic, and of cryptids most fearsome.

Vance Randolph (1892-1980) was well known as the leading folklorist of the Ozark region. Though not born there, Randolph spent the greater part of his adult life in the Ozarks, and a good portion of that life was devoted to gathering all the folklore, folk tales, and folk wisdom of the Ozark people. Randolph saw a way of life and a compendium of wisdom and belief that was quietly disappearing as modern advances made their way across the country, and he set out to chronicle as much of the old stories and knowledge as he could.

> *The Ozark region of Missouri and Arkansas has long been an enclave of resistance to innovation and "newfangled" ideas. Many of the old-time superstitions and customs have been nurtured and kept alive through the area's relative isolation and the strong attachment of the hillfolk to these old attitudes. Though modern science and education have been making important inroads in the last few decades, the region is still a fertile source of quaint ideas, observances, and traditions.*
> -Vance Randolph, Ozark Magic and Folklore

Randolph's printed collections of stories and old folk wisdom paint a picture of a region hidden from Time and the Outer World. The people of the Ozarks—especially those hillfolk of the farther reaches, some to this day living in a fashion that would seem primitive to the modern world—are full of superstitious belief and a healthy fear of and respect for the kind of natural magic that breathes forth from the hills themselves, a magic able to be harnessed only by those who remember the old ways.

> *Folk magic in the Ozarks has always been considered the work of the common people, born from the simple connection between the individual, their home, and the natural world around them.*

*-Brandon Weston, Ozark Folk Magic*

These hills and hollers are ancient, and the beliefs that simmer in their most remote areas are almost as old. Several Native American tribes made their home in the Ozarks, notably the Osage, Cherokee, and Quapaw. Those tribes had beliefs, traditions, and entities of their own, which were added to by the tales, traditions, and boogeyman of the European settlers who chose to eke out a living in the Ozarks' rocky, unforgiving soil. Those settlers were mostly Irish, Scottish, and German—all peoples known for their cultural treasure troves of spirts, specters, and things that go bump in the night.

*Spook Hollow: Tales of Ozark Horror* seeks to bring some of those stories, and those specters, to life. In these pages, you will find heartbreaking hauntings, hollow-eyed preachers, mysterious structures, wise old cats, nameless graves, cryptids—the Howler, the Gowrow, and more—and grannywomen aplenty.

So, grab your walking stick and strike out with us into the ancient forests, labyrinthine tunnels, and haunted, mist-filled hollers of the Ozarks. Bring your salt and your sage and your courage—you'll likely need all three.

# GRANNYWOMAN LIZ
## TEEL JAMES GLENN

"Tain't never cottoned to outsiders, no less Yankees tellin' me what to do, sonny," the wizened woman called Granny Liz said. "And I sure as hell ain't gonna let none traipse about up them hills." She waved a thin hand at a wooded section of the countryside. "Specially not where Cloud family bones is buried."

The Arkansas State Trooper who stood before her sighed. "I know, Liz."

"Miss Cloud," the silver-haired woman corrected. She was dressed in layers of blue and red gingham with a grey shawl tossed over her narrow shoulders, and at barely five feet tall she looked painfully small next to the burly officer.

"Miss Cloud, they are not going to hurt the land and they have a perfect legal right with documents from the state government to harvest turpentine."

"Ain't no government that can give no permission to desecrate graves—"

"They are not going to desecrate any graves, Miss Cloud," he said. "Turpentiners tap into the sap layers of the tree under the pine bark. The trees got something called oleoresin they put on the wound to protect it and seal the opening. Turpentiners channel the oleoresin into containers to make spirits of turpentine. They don't disturb the ground at all."

"They's walkin' on it, ain't they?" The old woman spat. "Yankee boots like yours walking on ground my pappy fought the bluecoats for."

"Now Miss Cloud, you know I ain't no Yankee. I come from less than fifty miles north of here. And the state can give turping rights to that Collin's Company, so don't be yelling at them no more."

The old woman squeezed her face into an unpleasant expression and tilted her head like a cat regarding a mouse. "The name of these mountains is made of two Choctaw words: *ouac*, their name for a buffalo, and *chito*, which is large." She looked up at the trooper and then waved a gnarled hand at the plains and hills around them. "When my pappy's pappy came out here there were still herds of those animals."

She walked past the officer to a wooden statue of a distinguished, middle-aged man in full confederate officer's uniform looking out over the flat land of the hollow. It was aged by weather but even a casual glance could see that the features of the man depicted bore a striking resemblance to the old woman.

"White men saw only something to conquer and kill. Greedy hunters killed them for their hides, left their bones to bleach in the sun and the meat to rot." The woman continued, "Eastern and northern folks pushed their way past here heading to the rich lands to the west, taking what they wanted. They still tryin'."

"Now, Granny Liz," the trooper said, "they just want to slash a few trees for the sap; people need the money—things are bad outside these hills since the crash of '29."

"Ain't no crash for those what work with their hands," the woman countered.

# GRANNYWOMAN LIZ

"Then you don't need that shotgun you was pointing at them boys down in the hollow," the trooper said. When she turned back to squint at him, he smiled. "I will talk to them about staying on the other side of the stream."

She made a noise like a cat hissing, but his smile stayed fixed and she accepted it as a peace offering. She pulled out a corncob pipe and a match from a dress pocket and lit up.

"Governor's paper ain't no real right, but if they stay over the stream I won't pepper 'em with shot."

"Miss Cloud, I will have to ask you not to pepper them at all," he said. "Even if they do stray on your side of the stream. Call me."

She glared at him in an attempt to make his smile crack but finally nodded. "But mark my words, Vernon Stuckie," she said. "I knowed you when you was barely in long pants—don't you lie to me."

"I promise, Miss Cloud, as long as you promise to not shoot anyone." He tried a stern look at her but smiled when she just turned her back to head toward her ramshackle log cabin.

"Pick up some of my peach preserves 'fore you leave, boy," she said. "But leave my squirrel gun alone."

"The trooper is leaving the old hag's place now, Mister Collins," Henry Duck said as he lowered the field glasses from his eyes. "He took something with him into his patrol car."

"Did you see what it was?" Joe Collins, unlike his foreman, was a thin man, almost delicate of features and with long thin fingers that he drummed against his thighs constantly. He was not dressed for the woods like Duck.

"No, sir," Duck said. "Maybe a box or something."

"Back country bribe," Collins said with disgust. "Pigs feet or some other delicacy."

"You got the governor's paper, boss; the law's gotta back you up."

"Not down here. These rubes stick together." He scowled.

"So how do we handle it, boss?" The deformed ear and scar tissue under Duck's eyes were souvenirs of his failed ring career, and his accent and his attitude were from the streets of Chicago's South Side.

"Same way you handled it in Florida," Collins said as he picked burrs from his pants before getting into his cream-colored coupe. "That old bag has the best pine trees in this whole area, along those flats. I want them all cut and bleeding for us by the end of the month or we'll lose the season."

"Won't that state cop get suspicious if we say we shot her in self-defense after he talked to her?"

The delicate Collins paused at his picking. "No reason to go that far—yet."

Duck put the binoculars up to his eyes and studied the clearing where Elizabeth Cloud's cabin and outbuildings were located.

Duck gave a gap-toothed smile. "That dump looks pretty rickety to me, boss. Seems like an old lady like that could knock over a candle or maybe fall asleep smoking in bed, ya know?"

Collins paused, foot on the running board, to listen.

"I was thinking that a good Samaritan who was maybe working across the stream close by might see the fire and manage to save her, but not the house, ya know? The old bag of bones would have to move out, but would be, ya know, grateful and all."

"Have I mentioned that you are a gem, Mister Duck?" Collins smiled. "A regular diamond in the rough."

Elizabeth Cloud had lived in the valley at the foot of the Devil's Backbone her whole life. She had been born on a farm down in the valley.

Arlan, her oldest brother, had died fighting the European war that was supposed to end all wars. Josephus, next oldest, had been killed in a bar fight with one of the Gillie brothers; that had started a feud that took Micah, the youngest, before her paw and cousins had killed the four Gillies and ended it.

Micah's death had taken the heart out of her mother, who withered away and died shortly after. Elizabeth's father followed her a few months later.

That was when Old Granny Jenny had taken in Elizabeth as her full-time apprentice and knew she was destined to be a grannywoman.

Elizabeth had moved into Jenny's cabin toward the older woman's end and had stayed almost eighteen years.

In that time the surrounding valleys had come to rely on Granny Liz when sicknesses came on them, when children were to be born, or when there was suspicion (or need) of a curse. She grew her own vegetables and herbs and gathered many rare plants for her poultices and potions. Things like skunk salve for clearing congestion and tea made from tubers of the Barnyard Blue Flower for soothing colic.

It was inherited knowledge from the frontier immigrants who brought European herbal knowledge and learned from the native tribes along the way. There were also secrets beyond medicinals; dark secrets that lurked in the shadows that no pastor would ever speak about at the pulpit.

Everyone in the Ozarks knew the power of the grannywomen and so they were both respected and feared—and tacitly ignored—by the men of the cloth.

Not so much outsiders.

State Trooper Vernon Stuckie found Mr. Collins was at the Arkansas House, a steakhouse two blocks from the office.

"Ah, Trooper Stuckie," Collins said with a wide smile. "What a coincidence you chowing down here." The table before the slight man was laden with enough food for three men the trooper's size.

"I'm afraid I'm here to talk to you about the turpentine collection down on the bottoms over at the Backbone."

"What about it, Officer?" The businessman held a glass of beer in one hand.

"Your man had trouble today with old Miss Cloud."

"Oh, yeah," Collins said. He motioned for the officer to sit at an empty chair at the table. "The old woman pulled a gun on my guys."

"More a force of nature," the trooper said as he sat. "And she did brandish a gun at them, but I have her assurances that will not happen again."

"Well good, it's nice to see my tax dollars are doing their work—"

"But there is a slight complication."

"Complication?" The businessman paused in the process of pushing a piece of steak into his mouth. "What complication? I got permits from the state to have my boys cut all those trees on the state land down there in the hollow."

"Yes, technically, you do, sir," Stuckie said. "But the survey lines of the state land extend to the west side of the little stream that runs through that hollow. Quite a ways, in fact."

"So? I got rights to tap the trees there."

"Yes," the trooper said. "Technically. But the folks here abouts do things a little less formally—the state park line was never really marked so they got kinfolk buried on that land."

"So? We ain't strip mining the place, just cuttin' some trees."

"Well, she still sees it as—well, kinda sacrilegious."

The businessman set down his drink and his fork and leaned forward. "It ain't no such thing; it is legal and I expect you to enforce the law. That bottom land is prime for turp-sap and I want it all."

"And I will," Stuckie said with bite in his tone. "I've gotten Miss Cloud to agree to not bother any of your men as long as they stay on the East side of the stream—"

"But we—"

"I know you have the right," the lawman continued. "But it will keep peace if you stay east. Leave that land for last and let me work on her some more. I'm sure we can resolve this peacefully."

Collins sat back in his chair and picked up his beer. "Yeah." He smiled before he took a deep draught of his beer. "No bloodshed. Sure, I'm a reasonable guy. We can start in the other sections and that'll give you plenty of time to convince the old hag. Sure."

"I see you," Granny Liz called. "Come out of there, you varmint." The woman took out her pipe and waved it at the smokehouse. "Don't make me come over there to get you."

There was a low, rumbling sound and then a dark shadow detached itself from the shed and slunk toward her on four legs.

"You dumb hound dog," she hissed. "I'll bet you didn't even catch that coon, did you, Jefferson Davis?" The dog came up to stand on the woman's left, ignoring the cat, who still stood on her right.

"I have to head over to little Ginny's tomorrow and make up a love spell for her on that boy Joe. But now, I suppose you want some supper, eh, boy?" She reached down and patted the dog on his massive shoulders which elicited a *woof* of affirmation. "You just wait out here; I got some soup bones I figured you'd want."

She went in the cabin to get the food and did not notice that the dog's ears pricked up and he took to sniffing the air as the wind shifted.

Out of the circle of the clearing, hidden in the trees, Henry Duck crouched in the underbrush and thought, "Okay, tomorrow sometime there'll be my chance. Sleep tight, lady," before he snuck away into the night.

Granny Liz was able to get the hair she needed from Joe to use in her charms without him knowing it. The woman rode her mule back to her own cabin.

"Sparkin' is natural," she said aloud to the mule. "But sometimes, Ulysses, I swear humans do it the most unnatural way!"

Ahead she could see some of the turpentiners moving through the woods and she squinted hard to see just where they had set their soaks for gathering the sap.

"Still on their side of the stream, Ulysses," she said aloud and scratched the mule on the neck. "I guess that Stuckie boy got through to them."

She urged the animal down the path to her clearing with thoughts of how she could help Ginny, so she didn't see Henry Duck slip from the cabin into the bushes on the other side of the clearing.

She didn't see him as he watched from the cover of the foliage, nor did she see the empty container of coal oil he carried that he had used to soak the firewood by her hearth.

Granny Liz opened the door to her cabin and was puzzled when Jefferson Davis did not come barking to greet her.

"Where are you, Mister President?" she called, becoming concerned.

The dog came slinking out of a corner, his head bowed and walking stiffly.

"Boy!" She moved quickly to the animal. He whimpered as she held his head and looked into his eyes, studying them.

"You look like you've been at my corn squeezins," she said. "Or elst you're powerful sick."

# GRANNYWOMAN LIZ

Granny Liz helped the dog over to her bed where she pulled him up on to it, lighting an oil lamp to be able to look more closely at the eyes of the ailing dog.

"What you been into, Mister President?" She sniffed his mouth and her features darkened as she looked around her cabin with a concerned eye.

"Or maybe I oughta say, 'what's been into you'?"

Henry Duck stood with one of his turpentining crew trying not to look like he was watching the old woman's house.

"We're almost done with this whole section, boss," the worker said to Duck. "We're ready to cross that stream tomorrow." The rough fellow glanced toward Granny Liz's cabin. "And some of the boys ain't very anxious to face that old bitty with a gun again."

Duck took a long drag on a cigarette before he answered. "I don't think that will be problem, Matt."

"You mean that Mister Collins got it all worked out with her?"

"Not to worry, Matt. The boss has ways of making problems disappear. Legally all those trees over there are on government land and ours to tap."

"If she don't shoot us."

"Grow a pair, Matt. She won't be a problem for much longer. Just have'ta wait till she gets hungry."

"Hungry?"

"Or when it gets dark enough." Duck chuckled. "Any time now."

Just as he spoke there was a brilliant flare of light from the other side of the grannywoman's cabin.

"There ya go," Duck said as he spat out his cigarette and started running toward the cabin. "Time for me to be a hero!"

The burly Duck ran just fast enough for his men to see that he was 'trying' to help. He made sure that the men were following him for them to be able to tell the State Troopers and his boss Collins that he had tried to save the old woman.

It would make things much simpler if the old woman was out of the picture and Henry Duck didn't care if she was hurt or dead, either way she would be off the grounds for more time than they needed to strip the turp sap from all the trees.

*And that is bonus money for me*, Duck thought as he rounded the corner of the cabin. There, Duck stopped, stunned by what he saw.

Six feet in front of the cabin the old woman was standing in front of a pile of cord wood that was blazing! When she heard Duck run up behind her, Granny Liz turned and smiled.

"Why, hi, y'all. What's the fuss all about?"

The other turpentiners ran up while Duck was still trying to find words.

"Cat got ya tongues, boys?"

"Uh, we thought something was wrong, ma'am." Matt said. "Least wise, Henry here did, and we figured he was right. We saw the flash fire—"

"Oh that," Liz said with a chuckle. "Seems some of my heating wood somehow got coal oil all over it and I just couldn't dare burn it in the house." She tottered over toward Henry Duck and then seemed to stumble so that she bumped into him. "Sure seems a terribly careless thing to put coal oil on firewood, don't it, fella?"

She fixed Henry in her glare and her smile took on a dark aspect. "Good thing my nose is still a sniffin' marvel, elst I would'a been cooked like a quail!"

She steadied herself and regarded all the roughnecks who had run to her aid.

"I 'preciate you gents all caring enough to come runnin'; if'n you'll sit yourself a moment I have some nice cool suntea for you all."

# GRANNY WOMAN LIZ

The men all looked around to each other, embarrassed, then a few smiles cracked and rough demeanors faded to shy smiles as they all surrendered to the offer of a cool, sweet drink.

Granny Liz kept a smile on her face as she served them and was particularly attentive to the burly Duck, refilling his cup.

Her change in attitude puzzled the foreman, and by the time she had collected all the cups and wished the men well he became more than puzzled. He began to feel a little fear.

"You bumbling fool!" Collins yelled at the towering foreman when Duck arrived at the office in Greenwood. "I told you to find a way to make her grateful to you so we could get tapping rights from her."

"Or make sure she wasn't able to object," Duck said. He did his best not to be cowed by the smaller man. "I figured it would work out one way or the other."

"Well, did it?"

"I-I don't know. She was weird."

"Weird?"

"I mean—I think she knew I was the one that poured the oil on the wood, but—"

"You don't think," Collins said. "Of course, she figured out you did it, she smelled the coal oil on you. I still can." He rose and paced the room.

"Okay, knucklehead," Collins finally said. "Here's what you're gonna do. I didn't want to go this far, but you've made sure we have to." He turned to stab the glowing end of a cigar at the burly foreman. "You're gonna knock that old bitty out and burn the place to the ground."

"But you just told me that I was wrong…"

"Shut up!" Collins screamed. "You were wrong because you failed. But we can make this work for us—the guys saw you try to help and heard her say she was careless with coal oil. So tonight, she gets careless again."

The little boss laughed. "You're even gonna bring the lady a nice gift in the morning, maybe a nice pie from that bakery down the block here for her being so nice with her tea."

Duck looked at his employer for a long moment, and then his coarse features split in a malicious grin. "Yeah, I'm a regular saint, ain't I?"

Granny Liz was busy after all the turpentiners went on their way. She hummed to herself as she took the few hairs she had secured from Henry Ducks's head and worked them into the head of a wax poppet.

The poppet had been fashioned from a carved root, paper, wax, and clay that had been stuffed with herbs.

She pressed Duck's hair into the crown of the figure she had fashioned to resemble the turpentiner.

She hummed old songs that Granny Jenny had taught her as she worked, using sage to give the air of the tiny cabin the aspect of a temple.

She sang to herself as she worked; an old tune about the Angel of Death.

*"I will sing of the twelve.*
*What of the twelve?*
*Twelve of the twelve apostles,*
*'Leven of the saint that has gone to Heaven,*
*Ten of the ten commandments."*

The poppet she placed in the center of the circle, and she sprinkled it with powdered animal bone and herbs in an ancient pattern she had learned at Jenny's knee.

When she finished she was exhausted, her lined face a mask of concentration.

"That's a good night's work, eh, Mister President?" she said to the dog.

# GRANNYWOMAN LIZ

The animal had rested quietly while she worked but now his head shot up, his ears perked and his head turned to stare at the door.

"I guess I done my fixin' just in time, boy. Seems we got visitors."

Henry Duck parked his car over the hill and walked down the road silently toward Granny Liz's cabin. He had a bar of soap in a sock in his right jacket pocket, a favorite prison version of a sap that would allow him to render the old woman unconscious without leaving a mark. He gave a savage grin as he thought about showering with the soap afterward and 'getting rid of the evidence' for the next week shower by shower.

When he came in sight of the cabin he paused. There was smoke coming from the chimney and he saw no sign of the dog, which he assumed was inside with the woman.

"That could be a problem," he thought. "He might not take drugged meat from me again." He carried a coil of rope that he could use to hold an animal while he clubbed it. The soap/sock sap would work just as well on the dog, and no one would examine the burned body of an animal.

After checking his weapons, Duck moved purposefully to the door of the cabin and paused to knock.

"Come in, Mister Duck." Granny Liz's voice came muffled through the door and made the burly thug jump.

He scowled, lifted the simple latch, and entered.

The old hound dog was seated by his mistress across the cabin and barely raised his head to acknowledge Duck's presence, save to growl.

"Hush, Mister President," the woman said. Granny Liz was seated in a high-backed chair with a comforter pulled around her shoulders. There was a roaring fire in the hearth, casting dancing shadows. "Do come in, Mister Duck."

The man entered, his hand in his jacket pocket resting comfortably on the improvised sap. He walked across the cabin slowly, mindful of the squirrel gun the woman had hanging over the fireplace.

"I… uh… I just wanted to see that you were alright, ma'am." Duck spoke haltingly as he stopped right in front of the old woman.

"I would ask you to sit down, Mister Duck," she said with a wide smile on her withered features, "but I think you will not be here that long."

He returned her smile with a dark tint. "Yeah, I'm pretty sure I won't be either." He slipped the sock out of his pocket and began to whirl it like a miniature lasso. "But then you won't be here much longer either."

The woman's reaction took the would-be-murderer completely by surprise; she laughed! A full-throated belly laugh until it brought tears to her eyes.

"Oh my, Mister Duck," she said when she could talk. "You really are a caution. You have a talent for seein' the future, ya know? You might almost be a grannywoman!"

Her reaction angered the burly thug and he raised the sap to strike at her, but suddenly his arm seemed to freeze in place. His muscles locked as if an invisible hand had grabbed his wrist to hold it.

"What the hell!"

"No reason to use profanity, young man. She rose from the chair and for the first time Duck could see that she was holding a small doll in her hand, one that he noticed was positioned just as he was at that moment.

"What the hell have you done to me?" There was fear in his voice. He grabbed his right hand with his left and tried to pull it down, but it was as unmoving as if it had been made of stone.

"Now you stop that talk!" She reached over to the poppet in her hand and pinched the small wax lips of the image. At that moment Duck's jaw seemed to lock. He moaned in terror.

"Oh, youngin'," she said with a shake of her head. "You is just as thin blooded as you are thick headed."

She moved to the hearth and procured a long taper, which she used to light her pipe.

Duck found he could not move at all save for his eyes, and they followed her movements. She puffed on her pipe while she regarded him.

"Did you really think you could pull the wool over Granny Liz's eyes, Mister Turpentiner?" She shook her head. "You city men think we mountain folk ain't got the sense God gave a coon, but it's you all that don't got a lick of sense. We know this land, we feel its pain, and you, comin' up here to rip the blood from our trees, scar up our land, you are the ones who will come to justice."

She puffed on her pipe and stroked her cat that had stretched and walked over to her, disdainfully stepping around the frozen Duck.

"But just what should that justice be, eh, Jonah?" She looked down at the cat that meowed to her in answer.

"Oh yes," the wisewoman said as if she understood the animal. "An excellent idea; just like the good book says, *an eye for an eye*!"

Trooper Vernon Stuckie drove his patrol car up to the foot of the road near Granny Liz's clearing. The early morning mist was still crawling along the hollow with a dream-like quality.

"I expect you to stand up for my legal rights, Officer," Joe Collins said. The little man was bundled in a trench coat that seemed as if it had been borrowed from his big brother.

"I will do my job, Mister Collins," the trooper said sharply. His breath puffed into cold mist. "I don't need you to tell me what it is."

"I know this old woman had something to do with my crew leaving yesterday and that voids any absurd agreement you made with her."

The trooper stopped short and turned to look down at the turpentiner. "I made a bargain in good faith, Mister Collins, and there is no proof that Miss Cloud had anything to do with your men leaving."

"There is no way that my foreman just up and left."

The two men halted when Jefferson Davis began to bark.

"Miss Cloud!" the officer called out. "I'd like to speak to you."

The dog stayed by the cabin but continued to bark until the grannywoman came out the door. "Hush, Mister President. Who is it?"

"It's me, Miss Cloud," the officer said. "Trooper Stuckie."

"Who's that with you?"

"I am Joseph Collins, Miss Cloud, I came here to find out what happened to my foreman, Henry Duck. And what you did to my men!"

The old woman walked slowly across the clearing while lighting her pipe. "Mister Collins," she said with a wide smile on her withered face. "I have been wanting to meet you."

"Morning, Miss Cloud," Trooper Stuckie said.

"Morning, Vernon," she said. She came to stand by the two men, dwarfed by the trooper but almost eye-to-eye with the shorter Collins.

"Madam—" Collins began.

"I ain't no madam, I'm Miss Cloud."

"Miss Cloud, what do you know about Mister Duck's disappearance?"

"Disappearance? Did he go somewhere?"

"You know damn well he's gone somewhere," Collins said. "My whole crew took off yesterday with a cock and bull story about hives or something."

"Watch your language, young man," the old woman said. "Don't you blaspheme near me."

"I say any damn thing I want; I got paperwork here that allows me to tap any of the trees right up to the property line and this officer is here to see that you abide by the law."

"I'll thank you not to put any words in my mouth and to keep a civil tongue in your head," Stuckie said. "I'm sorry, Miss Cloud, but there is some concern about Mister Collins' workers. Seems they all called in sick yesterday with some sort of rash and were sick to their stomachs."

"Oh, how very unfortunate; they all seemed just fine when they came to visit me day before yesterday and had a cool drink with me." She puffed out a cloud of smoke and then studied it as it blew away. "Maybe I got me some ointment that can help them."

"I don't need no hick quack messin' with my guys," Collins yelled. "I want what's comin' to me."

The old woman laughed softly. "Oh, I'm sure that will be a just solution here in the mountains."

At that moment a breeze came up from the hollow, blowing off the last of the fog and rustling the leaves of the foliage. The wind made a sound then like the low moan of a tormented soul.

That was when the trooper made an observation.

"Excuse me, Miss Cloud," the officer said, "but when did you get a second statue?"

Standing next to the carved wooden statue of Granny Liz's ancestor was a second figure, a crude wooden form that had the rough appearance of a modern working man dressed in a jacket and fedora with his hand raised above his head.

Collins shivered when he noticed the features on the new statue; they were in the exact image of Henry Duck. Most remarkable about the figure was that it was so life-like that you could almost see the fear in the eyes.

"I'm always acquirin' things," the old woman said. She fixed the turpentiner's eyes with hers. "You never know, I might just want to add to my collection again."

# THREE STEPS PAST THE ELM

## FENDY S. TULODO

The first thing that made the air feel wrong wasn't the heat... it was the boy's headless body dragging a long stick like it still had somewhere to be.

We didn't talk about what happened after that first hike. Not to anyone. Not to our Scout leader, not to the other kids, and especially not to each other. We all knew what we saw... but also didn't. That's how things work around here.

It was July, early morning, Camp Ashbrook near Newton County. Not the kind of place most tourists would find on a map, but enough of us local kids came here every summer for its dumb little hiking badges and overboiled chili. My name's Reed. Fourteen years old, and that whole week felt unbearable. Then came the final day—suddenly everything made sense.

The Ozarks are weird. That's not a joke. The hills breathe. Creaking trees break silence without wind. Alone, yet never feeling solitude. Some kids love that. I didn't.

Me and Cody had been bunkmates for two years. He was two years younger than me but taller. Stronger too. The kind of kid who acted like he'd been forty since birth. Proving people wrong thrilled him, even unasked. My initial dislike faded after that first storm. When his flashlight died, we used my spare. No jokes came—just a quiet "thanks" from him. That was rare for Cody.

Derrick was the third one. Quiet. Wrote in a sketchbook most nights. His tent was three down from mine. His parents were some kinda folklore researchers, I think. He was always reading stuff no one else cared about. Old papers, weird local ghost stories, Ozark myths about things with names nobody could say right. I used to call him "National Geographic," but after that week, I stopped joking.

That morning, our Scoutmaster, Mr. Pelkins, told us to head out before the sun got high. Said the trail was called Elm Stretch. Said we'd know it by the triple-trunked elm tree. "Just three miles out and three back. Easy trail. Follow the signs, stick together," he said, sipping from a coffee cup that smelled like bourbon and gum.

We packed up, grabbed our maps, and left in pairs. Me, Cody, and Derrick split from the group early because Cody said he saw something move near the trail's bend. Said he was sure it was a raccoon or a fox.

We shouldn't've followed him.

The elm stood about fifteen feet tall, three trunks knotted from one base, curved like something once tried to rip them apart but gave up halfway. A rusty chain hung between two of the trunks. Looked like a clothesline but older, with metal clips that rattled in the wind. Nobody touched it.

"Three steps past the elm," Derrick muttered, not looking at us.

# THREE STEPS PAST THE ELM

"What?" I said.

"There's an old story. The third step after the elm is where things aren't yours anymore. Your path. Your mind. Your shape. Ozark witch belief... sorta like stepping past your own grave."

Cody laughed. "Cool. Bet it's haunted by your notebook."

I ignored them both and kept walking. I counted the steps out loud, probably to annoy them, probably because I felt something wrong too.

"One... two... three..."

That was when it got colder. Like... too fast. Like someone opened a fridge on the trail. My neck tightened, and the sounds... stopped.

No birds. No insects. No crunching gravel.

I turned around to say something dumb, maybe a joke, maybe to ask if they felt that too. But Derrick was gone.

And Cody was staring at something behind me.

I spun fast. At first I thought it was just a tree stump. Black, cracked, not moving.

Then it... moved.

The thing was shaped like a person, mostly. Except there was no head. Just a long neck, like it had been pulled too far and sealed shut at the top, raw and bulging like meat that tried to heal wrong. It had arms, long ones, like they weren't connected right. The hands dragged behind it, knuckles cracked open like dry bark.

It wore part of a Scout uniform. That was the worst part.

A sash. A torn yellow neckerchief. One shoe.

The thing lifted its headless body, sniffed or... something. Then it dragged a thick stick behind it, like a walking cane. But it wasn't walking. It was pacing.

Cody backed up. "What... what the..."

The rock caught his foot—down he went, crashing hard.

That sound... that must've made it notice us. Its body twitched. It turned... not like a person, more like it rotated from the waist. Then it moved fast.

Not toward Cody. Toward me.

I didn't scream. I couldn't. My legs didn't wait for instructions.

I ran.

Through brambles. Past trees I didn't recognize. My lungs burned as my legs drove forward. Greens and browns smeared together, the world dissolving into a watery mess around me.

Then I fell.

It wasn't deep, the fall. But my face landed in something sticky. At first, I thought it was sap. But it was too red. And too warm.

I blinked. Took in the clearing.

There were clotheslines here. Dozens. Rusty chains stretched between trees like webbing. And every chain held... uniforms.

Scout uniforms.

Shirts. Shorts. Necklaces. Pins.

Torn. Weathered. Some fresh.

Shoes still had feet in them.

I dry-heaved, crawling backward into a bush, tearing my elbow on a broken tin box. I didn't stop.

Then I heard Cody.

"Reed! Here! This way!!"

His voice echoed weird. Too loud, too close.

I turned. He stood behind me.

"I saw where it went," he said.

His face looked too calm.

I blinked again. Something didn't sit right.

His shoes. One was missing.

The exact one I saw on that thing.

I froze. "Where's Derrick?"

He smiled. It didn't reach his eyes.

"Oh, he's fine. He stayed behind. Said he wanted to write this down."

My heart thundered. I knew Cody. And this... wasn't him.

"Take a step forward," I said. Quiet. Testing.

He did. His foot made no sound.

None.

Not even a crunch.

The leaves under him didn't move.

I turned and ran again.

Eventually, I found the trail signs. Real ones. Wooden, etched in old paint. I followed them, breath hitching, throat raw. I don't know how long I ran. Maybe hours.

When I got back to camp, it was nearly sunset.

Kids were eating beans near the fire pit. Laughing. Mr. Pelkins poured something into his thermos. Normal. Too normal.

I stood at the tree line, filthy, bleeding, shaking.

No one noticed.

Except Derrick.

He was sitting on a stump near the flagpole, sketching.

I stumbled over. "Where... were you?!"

He looked up, eyes wide. "Dude. I've been back for hours."

"What?! That thing... Cody... he... "

"Wait." Derrick held up a hand. "Cody?"

I stopped.

"He's... he's not here?"

"No," Derrick said slowly. "He never made it back. I thought he doubled back to help you."

My knees buckled. "Then who... who talked to me?"

Derrick looked down at his sketchpad.

Then he flipped it toward me.

It was a charcoal drawing.

Of me.

Standing alone.

And behind me... the headless thing, holding Cody's face like a mask.

"Wait... did you draw this before or after I showed up?" I asked.

Derrick didn't answer.

I grabbed the sketchpad and flipped through it. Page after page... all charcoal, all fast strokes, smudged fingerprints, and jagged lines. He had drawn the woods. The chains. The triple elm. And me.

Always me.

Sometimes with Cody. Sometimes without.

Sometimes... with something behind me, staring.

"You knew," I said, voice cracking.

"No." He stood up, grabbing the sketchbook back. "I didn't know. I dreamed it."

"What?"

"Last night. Maybe before. The drawings weren't mine. I woke up, and they were there. I thought I was drawing something made up."

"You didn't think to say something?!"

Derrick glanced around. Kids laughing. Mr. Pelkins whistling some off-key song about beans or biscuits. Like nothing weird had ever happened here.

"Being the crazy kid again wasn't what I wanted."

My fists tightened as I retreated. "Cody's being worn by that thing like some cheap suit."

Derrick nodded slowly. "I think it's older than all of us. Older than this camp."

I turned and stormed off toward our tent. I needed to sit down. I needed to breathe. I needed to find Cody's pocket knife.

He always left it beside his pillow, under a folded camp towel. The one with "Pack 24" sewn into the corner.

When I got there, the towel was gone.

So was the knife.

And something had scratched the side of the tent with a stick.

Three straight lines. Deep. Fresh.

That night, I didn't sleep.

No one noticed Cody missing. No one asked.

I sat up, flashlight in one hand, pocket Bible in the other. Not 'cause I was religious... just because my mom packed it and I didn't want to feel alone.

Around two a.m., I heard movement.

But not from outside.

From the bunk above mine.

The bunk Cody used.

There was weight shifting. Springs creaking.

Then a slow sound... like cloth tearing.

I froze.

The flashlight shook in my hand.

The weight shifted down. I saw fingers curl around the bunk rail.

Long ones.

Too long.

A shape lowered itself halfway, like someone peeking over the edge. I aimed the light... and my breath stopped.

Cody's face. But wrong.

Too pale. No freckles. The eyes were wide, black, no whites. Like glass.

And the smile...

It wasn't smiling with his mouth. It was smiling with the skin. Like a mask stretched across something else.

"Reed," it said, in his voice.

Flat. Dry. Like playback through a broken speaker.

"Come with me. I found where it sleeps."

I bolted.

I didn't care about the flashlight. I ran in socks across gravel and dirt, scraped my toes, sliced my ankle on a broken badge pin. I didn't stop.

I ran straight to Derrick's tent and dove in like my life depended on it.

Because it did.

Derrick sat up instantly. "What happened?!"

"It was... Cody. No. Not Cody. It's using him... I don't know... It... It talked to me."

"Okay. Okay. Breathe."

He clicked on a lantern. The kind with the plastic green top and fake candle inside. I hated the color of the light. Sick yellow. It made shadows look alive.

"You said you read about this stuff," I whispered. "Anything like this before?"

He hesitated. "Maybe."

From his sleeping bag, he pulled out a folded map. Not the camp one. This was hand-drawn. Black ink. With lines that zigzagged across the hills. Symbols. Circles. Notations in tiny handwriting.

"What is this?"

"My dad found it years ago. Didn't believe it. Thought it was a prank by some ranger. But then... stuff started happening."

"Like?"

"Missing hikers. Reports of people showing up twice. You get it? Like... someone already came back. But then another version of them did too. Both remembered things. Slightly wrong."

"What's that got to do with Cody?"

He tapped one corner of the map. "This symbol. See it? Three hooks. That's the chain tree. The triple elm."

He paused.

"That's where it starts."

"What starts?"

"The duplication. The feeding. The... hunting."

The lantern dimmed suddenly. I grabbed it. Shook it. But the light stayed low.

Then we heard something outside the tent.

Not footsteps.

Dragging.

Slow. Steady. Like wood being pulled through gravel.

"Okay, okay," Derrick whispered. "It knows."

"No kidding."

I reached for a pen knife in my sock. It was dull. Could barely cut string. But it felt better than nothing.

"I have a plan," Derrick said. "You're not gonna like it."

"Try me."

"We go back to the elm."

"Nope. Hard pass."

"Listen. That thing showed up *after* we passed it. Something about that spot started this. If we cross it again, we reverse it."

"That's dumb."

"So is staying here waiting to get flayed alive in your tent."

Fair point.

We waited until the dragging sound faded.

Then we ran again. This time with our packs, flashlights, and whatever junk we thought might help: salt packets, duct tape, half a sandwich, a compass, and Derrick's map. My hand shook every time it brushed the rough paper.

We passed the fire pit. Still hot.

Passed the bathrooms. Still stinking.

And back into the woods, straight toward the elm.

We didn't talk.

We just moved.

When we got there... the elm looked different.

Taller. Hungrier.

The chains were missing.

Instead, they were *wrapped* around something standing next to the tree.

It looked like a person.

But there were too many arms.

And the face...

It was Cody's.

And Derrick's.

And mine.

Layered. Blinking out of sync.

Breathing.

We froze.

A sudden lurch twisted my gut. Pressure built in my ears, muffling sounds as if submerged.

"What... is that?" I whispered.

Derrick's hand trembled. "It's all of us. It's a memory. No... it's what it *wants* us to become."

The creature tilted. A rope of chain unraveled and hissed across the ground toward our feet.

I stepped forward.

Derrick grabbed me. "Are you crazy?!"

"Three steps, right?"

He blinked. "You're serious?!"

"One..."

"Reed, don't!"

"Two..."

"REED!!"

"Three."

The forest exploded.

Not literally... but it felt like it. My body bent in every direction. My ears popped. The wind screeched.

But the creature...

It stumbled.

Like someone yanked out its battery.

The face peeled back. The chains hissed like snakes dropped in acid. It collapsed into the roots of the elm, melting into the dirt, dragging the masks with it.

And then... it was gone.

No wind. No sound. Just us. Standing there. Staring at the tree like it was the end of something.

Derrick exhaled. "What... what did you do?"

"I reset it."

He blinked.

"You said the third step opens the curse. So I figured... stepping again might close it."

"That's not how magic works."

"Worked today."

Derrick dropped to his knees, laughing.

# THREE STEPS PAST THE ELM

It wasn't happy laughter. It was tired. Relieved. Broken.
Then he pointed.
On the ground, near the base of the tree...
Cody's sash.
Torn. Dirty. Real.
And nothing else.
We buried the sash.

Not because it made sense. Not because it would help. We buried it because it felt like the only decent thing left to do.

Used a rock to dig, near the triple elm. Didn't say anything while we did it. I didn't pray. Neither did Derrick. We were both thinking the same thing:

If this thing could wear Cody's face... what if it could wear *ours* next?

We walked back to camp slowly. Birds were chirping again. That creepy too-perfect kind of chirping, like someone pressed play on a fake nature soundtrack.

"I don't trust this," I muttered.

"Yeah," Derrick said. "Too normal."

When we reached the campgrounds, everything *looked* the same.

Tents still up. Campers still laughing. Smoke still rising from the fire pit.

Mr. Pelkins waved us over like nothing happened.

"There you boys are! Hiding from kitchen duty, huh?" he said, slapping the side of his thermos.

We stared.
He stared back.

"You two alright? You look like you got chased by the devil."

Derrick looked at me.

A slow shake of my head answered first.

My lips stretched, unnatural. "Yeah," came out. Too bright. "All good here."

Because if we told him, he'd think we were nuts.

Or worse...

He'd already been replaced too.

That night, we kept watch. Took turns sitting at the edge of our tent with flashlights pointed at the woods.

Nothing happened.

Until 3:04 a.m.

That was the exact time I heard *him*.

"Reeeeeed... come help me... I'm lost..."

It was Cody's voice.

Not warped. Not fake.

Not monster-Cody.

Actual Cody. Tired. Crying. Like he was dragging his leg.

The voice came from the woods, past the path.

I clenched the flashlight. "Derrick. He's calling me."

"I know."

"I have to go."

"No, you don't."

"What if it's *really* him?"

Derrick's voice cracked. "It's *not*."

The voice came again.

Louder.

This time from behind us.

"REEED—IT'S DARK—I CAN'T FEEL MY LEGS—"

I snapped the zipper, stumbled outside, scanned the dark with shaking hands.

Nothing.

Derrick grabbed my arm. "Do you know what this is?"

I didn't answer.

"It's bait. You buried the sash, right? You cut its link. Now it needs *you* to give it a new one."

The voice stopped.

And from the treeline...

A shape stepped out.

It was Cody.

But only on the outside.
He was smiling.
Grinning so wide it looked painful.
And he was holding something.
His own *face*.
Like a mask in his hand.
I screamed.
Not out loud. My voice didn't work.
I dropped the flashlight. My legs barely moved.
Derrick raised his lantern. "BACK UP!"
The thing didn't flinch.
"BACK UP—GO BACK WHERE YOU CAME FROM!"
Then the thing's grin dropped.
It looked... disappointed.
Like a kid denied candy.
It tilted its head—well, where the head should've been—and whispered something I'll never forget.
"You're not supposed to *know* yet."
Then it melted into the dirt.
No wind. No exit. Just gone.
Derrick lowered the lantern. "We have to leave."
"Yeah."
"Now."
We packed before sunrise.
Didn't say goodbye to anyone. Left our mess kits, our trail maps, everything.
Just hiked.
Straight down the gravel road that led to the ranger station.
Halfway there, I looked back.
And there, at the top of a ridge, under the trees...
Cody was standing again.
Smiling.
This time, he didn't wave.

He lifted the sash.
Put it back around his neck.
And pointed at me.
Like a promise.
Like a warning.
I turned and didn't look back again.
We called our parents from the ranger office.
Told them camp was cut short, that we had stomach cramps, that we needed to go.
They believed us.
Or wanted to.
When my mom picked me up, she didn't ask many questions.
She never liked camp anyway.
Derrick's parents arrived an hour later. We nodded to each other before leaving.
No big goodbye. No hugs. Just a look.
Like soldiers getting discharged after a mission nobody talks about.
School started two weeks later.
No one talked about Cody.
When I asked around, they said his parents transferred him out mid-summer. No contact info. No new school listed.
His house had a For Sale sign.
Windows boarded.
Grass too long.
I rode my bike there one Saturday and stood on the sidewalk for ten minutes.
That's all I did.
Stand there.
The front door was open.
Not wide. But enough to tempt someone stupid.
I didn't go in.
But I saw something move inside.
Tall. Too tall.

I left fast.
Never went back.
A year passed.
Then one day, Derrick messaged me.
Said he found something.
"Same thing happened in 1972. Scout troop. Triple-trunked elm. One kid never came back. No reports. Just... disappeared."
He sent me a scan of a newspaper clipping.
BLACK BOG SCOUT ACCIDENT. One boy unaccounted. Search canceled after four days.
I looked closer at the photo.
Three boys in uniform.
One looked like Cody.
My stomach dropped.
I messaged Derrick back: "Did you notice the sash?"
He replied: "Yeah."
It was the same one.
Same fray. Same pattern.
Like it never aged.
I tried to forget.
Didn't work.
I deleted the message, deleted the photo. I even blocked Derrick for a few weeks, thinking maybe distance would help. It didn't.
Every night for two months, I had the same dream.
I'm standing in front of the triple elm.
The chains aren't hanging anymore... they're *weaving*.
Wrapping around something tall and headless that grows bigger every time I see it.
And every time, just before I wake up...
It pulls off my face.
Like it was trying to wear me next.

It wasn't until college orientation that I heard from Derrick again.

He'd transferred to a university two hours from mine. Sent me a text out of nowhere.

*You seeing this too?*

I called him right away. No small talk.

"Still dreaming?"

"Yeah," he said. "Only now... it's not just me. My girlfriend saw something in my dorm mirror. Said I stood behind her."

"You didn't?"

"I was in class."

I exhaled. "Okay... maybe it's waking up again."

"No. It *never slept.* We just left."

I paused. "Why call now?"

"Because I found out something else."

"What."

"I think there's *another tree.*"

We met in person that weekend. Drove three hours to a little Ozark town called Maple Hollow. It wasn't even on Google Maps. You had to know someone to even get the directions right.

We followed a hand-drawn route Derrick got from an old local man he met in a museum archive. Guy said "bad things grow in places people forget." I believed him.

The trail wasn't marked. We had to hike into thick brush. Not Elm Stretch this time... but somehow, it *felt* the same.

Same damp air. Same shift in wind. Same crunch that didn't echo.

And when we saw it...

Triple trunks again.

But not elm.

This one was *oak.*

Thicker. Older. Scarred.

Wrapped with barbed wire instead of chain.

And something else.

A sign.

Wooden. Faded.

Painted in red letters:

**"STEP AGAIN AND IT LEARNS YOUR NAME."**

We stopped ten feet away.

"Should we burn it?" I asked.

Derrick was silent.

"I mean it. Set the thing on fire, salt the roots, whatever makes it stay dead."

He shook his head. "Won't work."

"Why?"

"Because it's not about the tree."

I stared at him. "Then what is it?"

He looked at me—quiet, calm, and broken.

"It's about *us*."

That night, we camped just outside the trail's edge. Sleep refused to claim either of us.

Near the tree, a light appeared when the clock showed one.

Flickering. Like a lantern swinging.

I stood.

Derrick followed.

We walked slowly, flashlights off, breathing shallow.

And when we got close, I saw them.

Three figures.

Standing in front of the oak.

Not moving. Not talking.

I recognized one immediately.

Cody.

The other two...

Were us.

But younger.

Wearing the old uniforms. Covered in dirt. Faces pale, lips tight, eyes glassy like dolls.

"Don't move," Derrick said.

Too late. My younger self turned to look right at me.

And smiled.

Not sweet.

Not evil.

Just... tired.

Then it held up a chain.

Dropped it at our feet.

Turned back.

And all three of them... stepped into the tree.

Literally.

Like the bark swallowed them.

No sound. No blood. Just gone.

We left.

Didn't speak on the walk back.

Didn't speak on the drive home.

Didn't speak for months after.

But I knew what it meant.

It wasn't haunting us because we escaped.

It was waiting.

Because now it had our *shape*.

It had *our faces*.

It could wait as long as it needed.

Because one day, someone else would take three steps past a tree they didn't understand.

And it would *wear* them too.

Two years later, I went back one last time.

Alone.

Stood at the base of Elm Stretch.

The chain tree still there.

But thinner now.

Like it was fading.
Or... waiting to be fed again.
I dug up the sash.
It was dry. Clean. Untouched.
I studied it for what felt like hours. My fingers finally let go, sending it into the flames of our old meeting place.
Watched it burn.
And that night, for the first time since I was fourteen...
I slept without dreaming.
Next morning, I mailed Derrick a letter.
No return address.
One line only:
*"If it ever speaks in my voice, don't listen. That won't be me."*

# NSFW

## XAVIER POE KANE

The old man stepped outside his garage, the light illuminating the winter's night while the frigid arctic air bit at the exposed skin of his face. Nearby, his SUV beat a deep bass rhythm as it warmed itself against the bitter cold.

He looked at his phone. "Fucking weathermen," he cursed.

The night before, the phone had told him it would be cold and cloudy but without precipitation. The predicted dry, fluffy snow was supposed to move south of him. Instead, prickly, blowing snow on the cusp of turning to sleet was currently pelting him in the face, and an inch was already accumulating on the ground. The phone informed him this would be the case for the next six hours.

He shook his head and checked the text he'd gotten from his wife. She usually left even earlier than he did, and even on the summer solstice, she would leave before the sun rose.

Looks like Meramec Bottom gonna be closed soon.

The old man shook his head at the inconvenience of taking a longer route to work. He saw the three bouncing dots as she was typing.

At work. Love you!

His frown turned upside down. He dialed her work. "I'm calling it," he said as her angelic voice greeted him. "I'm calling in claiming N-S-F-W."

"N-S-F-W?" His wife's tone was one of confusion.

"Not safe for work." Pride for knowing the grandkid's lingo burst through his tone.

His wife giggled. "I don't think that means what you think it means."

"Well, what does it mean?"

Another giggle. "Something more… titillating. Anyway, staying home is a good idea," she agreed. "It wasn't that bad when I got in, but some of the guys who got in after me said it's getting pretty slippery out there."

"Yeah, if the branch chief isn't okay with work from home, I'm going to take PTO." He sighed his signature sigh that meant everything from defeat to defiance. "If things get worse, are you going to stay at your dad's tonight?"

"I was thinking so, if you'll be all right on your own."

"I think I'll make do." He hung up with a shiver.

Something tickled at the dormant part of his brain—the one that had last come alive when bow hunting back in 1998.

He'd been watching a trophy buck cautiously cross a field of tall grass, slowly coming within range of his lethal skill with the bow. It had repeatedly lifted its head from sniffing or scraping the ground for the last edible acorns of the season to stare in his direction as if it knew there was danger nearby.

He'd heard the breaking of limb and slowly surveyed the ground in the direction it came from. It had taken him a moment to make out the shape of the mountain lion against the woods. His hands had slowly moved to his .44 magnum revolver. Drawing the pistol, he'd shot, narrowly missing the endangered predator so that both he and the large cat could see another sunrise.

Turning back to the field, the trophy buck was long gone.

He'd told the story once to the amused disbelief of kith and kin. While mountain lions were rare in the Missouri Ozarks, they weren't unheard of. Unfortunately, they were still scarce enough that people looked upon stories without a carcass as just another tall tale. But the old man knew the truth, and that was good enough for him.

Discretion being the better part of valor, he opened his Lincoln Way app to shut off his car and call it quits. Turning his back on the darkest part of night, it was only when he was far enough inside the garage that his lizard brain stopped screaming "Run!"

He never noticed the two orbs of red watching him from the woods across the road.

The old man sat at his computer, trying to focus on work. Ever since he was a child, he'd loved snow days. However, his arthritic knees precluded tearing down the hill on the grandkids' plastic toboggan. Instead, he'd spend the day in his home office, snug and warm as he drank coffee and looked out over the five acres where he and his wife had built not only a home but a life.

They lived on the edge of civilization, their property line butting on the often swampy wetlands of the Meramec River on three sides. During the hunting season, he didn't need to go far for deer or turkey since the city folk who tromped through the public land would unwittingly run them toward him.

But such convenience came at a cost: It was an hour's commute to his work and forty-five minutes for his wife. Luckily, he had a good team that didn't need his presence and could operate without him if the powers that be required him to take leave.

He sent some emails and messages before languidly idling in the kitchen, making coffee and a hot breakfast instead of the usual cold cereal he choked down in his cubicle at the office. He took a moment to appreciate the space.

His wife had begged him for a remodel of the kitchen and their two baths. He hated renovating a house he was living in, but she was the best woman a man could hope to ever have as a partner, so he'd relented. And she was right to have done so.

They'd turned the once separate dining room and kitchen into an open concept: a large U-shaped kitchen with one arm featuring a sink that overlooked the backyard, the other allowing for bar-like seating whenever they had company, and a stove, microwave, and upper cabinets in the middle.

Special reverence was given to a large ceramic rooster—the only thing left from his bachelor days. They were alumni of the U of South Carolina, and he would forever be a Gamecock, or 'Cock for short.

He couldn't help but smile remembering his wife's butt in a tight pair of short-shorts with the word "Cocks" emblazoned on the back. She hated it, thought it was garish and made sure he knew it, but she was fair and its inclusion made him happy like the kitchen remodel had made her.

This kitchen was now one of his favorite places to be. Thinking ahead to lunch, he gathered some meat and veggies, a cutting board, and a ten-inch chef's knife to prepare a stew.

It was only 5:30 a.m. and still pitch black. He looked out the kitchen window, and he could see the faint light of his nearest neighbor in the distance.

Andrew McAlarney, or Mac, was an eccentric IT wunderkind who moved in right before the nation went into COVID lockdown. The guy could be weird and spout random stuff, but he was kindhearted and always there to help his elderly neighbors when they needed it.

Such help was returned when the old man drove Mac to chemotherapy after the cancer that got the younger man booted from the Air Force returned. Through chemo, the younger man had learned to love life and vowed to never touch a gun again.

Over the years, the old man came to love the newly pacifist Mac as a son. He thought about paying him a visit later after the sun had risen and if there was a break in the storm.

The barking of Daisy, his oldest dog, roused him from thoughts of socializing with his buddy. It was the same incessant bark that had kept him and his wife awake the past few nights. Some critter had been invading their yard, and Daisy and her son Chuck were none too happy about it.

"Fine, you want out in this bullshit? Have at it, fuckers," he said with equal parts amusement and condescension as they raced out the door and into the blinding snow.

Safe and warm, his eyes tried to pierce the darkness through the window while he sipped fresh coffee. He could make out the shapes of his dogs and something else—taller than a man and standing on two legs.

It moved in blurred motion as the animals leaped at it.

"It's a fucking bear!" the old man yelled as his faithful companions attacked the threat to their family. He flung the French doors open to scream, "Daisy! Chuck! Get your asses in here!"

The only answer was Chuck's painful yelp.

Heart pounding with rage, the old man rushed into his office. He kept an antique SKS rifle hanging on his wall, its bayonet extended in a display of malicious coolness. He grabbed the stripper clip he kept hidden for emergencies from behind some books.

Working the ancient action back, he slid the stripper clip into the guide and fed the rounds into the gun's internal magazine before tossing the empty clip aside and letting the bolt slam forward, chambering a round.

In his anger, he neglected to put on his parka or even boots before he rushed out the back door. Not feeling the bite of the icy snow as his thick socks sank into the accumulation, he shouldered his weapon and took aim where he last saw the bear.

The antique rifle only held ten rounds, but the old man was a marksman who thought that was nine more than he needed. Keeping his back to his home, he looked for trouble through the wind-swept snow. Something large scurried across his vision, obscured by the early morning darkness and shadows thrown by the kitchen lights. He fired.

Nothing.

A deep growl from his left made his heart stop.

He swung toward the sound, and a blur rushed at him. He fired and was this time rewarded by a satisfyingly angry cry of pain.

Still, the shadow continued its advance.

He fired again. In the instantaneous flash of the muzzle, he saw mangled black fur, a bloodied snout, and at least one demonic horn twisting upward from the beast's skull.

Once more shrouded by darkness, it growled, low and aggrieved. The fetid stench of death wafted as the creature approached.

Instinctively, the old man thrust the rifle forward, smiling in primal rage as the bayonet sank into the animal's flesh. The victorious moment soon ended as the beast howled in unmistakable fury.

A clawed backhand struck him against the chest, breaking several ribs and sending him flying against the house, where he crumpled into a heap on the ground. His breath was knocked out of him, and he desperately clung to consciousness.

With another frenzied howl, he saw his rifle go flying and land with a series of clattering thuds as it crashed through a nearby copse of trees.

Dazed, the old man stared into the snow. He was hurt and unprepared for the elements. If the demon didn't end his life, Mother Nature would.

As he scanned the night, his gaze settled upon two crimson orbs, rising in rhythm with the demon's panting. As the combatants watched one another, the old man realized he had only one chance to make the fifteen-foot dash to his back door. If only his arthritic knees would work, one last time.

Summoning all his courage and fortitude, he pushed himself off the ground and sprinted to safety.

The beast growled behind him—a deep snarling sound straight from a neanderthal's nightmare. It was punctuated by guttural gurgles as if it were exhaling liquid hellfire. The vocalizations were joined by the thumping sound of the large beast loping along on all fours as it quickly closed the distance between them.

The old man stumbled into his house and the imagined safety of his kitchen. He slammed the door behind him and grabbed the knife from where he'd left it on the cutting board. He spun around at the sound of shattering windows and was pelted by a rain of glass every bit as beautiful as it was dangerous.

Upon seeing his combatant face to face, he almost dropped the knife.

He had heard of the Ozarks Howler but had never put much stock in it or any other cryptid. That ancient monsters could hide in modern America made no sense to him, what with all the cameras that made up not only the surveillance state but were employed by homeowners to see who was at the door or hunters to track game.

But here was one, standing larger than life, in his own kitchen. It was at least seven feet tall, its face a chimera of bear and wolf with the addition of two hellishly large horns growing from its skull.

Staring down his likely death, his thoughts focused dumbly on the popcorn ceiling. It had been the object of several arguments between him and the wife over the course of the remodel. And now the popcorn floated down upon him as if it were indoor snow as the beast's horns dug great gouges in the ceiling.

Its body was covered in a tangled mess of black fur. Its arms terminated in a hybrid of paw and hand with long curved claws. The viscera from the old man's dogs still dripped from them.

However, the beast was also wounded. There was a long laceration where the SKS's bullet grazed him and a deep gash where he'd bayoneted the creature in its right pec. Its chest rose and fell as it panted from exertion and pain.

The pair of predators stared at each other in the space where lesser animals were routinely prepared for dinner.

Like a switch, the old man's mind focused on his predicament. In order for his wife to come home and his grandkids to ever visit again, this animal had to die.

Enraged at the killing of his canine best friends, the pain inflicted upon him, and the final insult of his home being invaded, the old man screamed. Ignoring the searing agony of his ancient joints and wanting the nightmare to end once and for all, he lunged.

The glowing red eyes of his target grew wide in momentary shock before narrowing as its own survival instincts kicked in, and it leaped to meet the threat.

The pair began a dance of claw and knife, of gnashing teeth and tearing flesh. It was a dance of death. The old man stabbed wildly, each thrust piercing the cryptid's mangy hide.

Blood splattered the kitchen as they slammed into cabinets. Appliances, dishes, and utensils smashed and clattered to the floor as they were knocked off the counter. But when the ceramic rooster went flying and smashed against the wall, time stood still.

As the tacky decoration disintegrated in a cloud of ceramic dust and chunky pieces that could never be put back together again, the old man felt his age. Every joint ached. His taut back muscles screamed as the adrenaline rush and fight for his life forced them to be more flexible than they'd been in a decade, maybe more.

Watching the last symbol of his youth destroyed and the honest acknowledgement of his body betraying him filled him with a desperate rage against the encroaching darkness of death.

With one final burst of strength, he hacked and slashed wildly at his attacker. "Fuck you! I'm not going down without a fight!" The Howler's blood splashed, bathing him in gore as his knife made long gashes in the creature's hide.

The beast took its pound of flesh as well. Claws disemboweled the old man, turning his insides into outsides. Teeth sank into his shoulders in an attempt to control what should've been an easy kill.

The snap of metal breaking off as half the knife remained inside the creature let the old man know he was done for. He was flung backward, his lower spine slamming against the granite countertop he and his wife had spent hours picking out.

His back twisted at an unnatural angle as he cried out in pain and dropped to the floor. He glared at the animal, its legs trembling, with blood spurting from one wound and oozing out of the rest.

Its red eyes seemed dim as it slowly backed out of the door and into the night.

The old man coughed a bubble of blood and stared at the broken door as he felt the life leaving his body. He closed his eyes and had begun to pray that death would come soon when he was interrupted by the sound of crunching glass.

Expecting to see the animal returning to finish him off, he was surprised to see that it was his young neighbor hurrying inside.

Mac was yelling at him, but his voice was distant. Still, the garbled words gave the old man the sense he was being implored to hold on and that help was on the way.

Smiling, he uttered his last words. "Mac… are you… holding… a fucking… wooden spoon?"

# WHO GOES WHERE?

## ANDREW KURTZ

The fog rolled through Devil's Backbone Ridge like the breath of something ancient and hungry, clinging to the hollows between the Arkansas hills with an unseasonable persistence that made the locals nervous. It was October, but the mist carried the chill of deep winter and the stench of something rotting in the creek beds below.

Joan Lamont pulled her jacket tighter as she stepped out of her rental car, the gravel crunching beneath her hiking boots with a sound like breaking bones. She'd driven twelve hours from Chicago to reach this godforsaken corner of the Ozarks, following a lead that had kept her awake for three straight nights.

The disappearances had started six months ago—hikers, hunters, even a few locals who knew these woods better than their own backyards. Eleven people vanished without a trace, leaving behind only shredded clothing and pools of blood that the Arkansas State Police couldn't explain.

As a freelance journalist specializing in unsolved mysteries, Joan had seen her share of bizarre cases. But something about the witness statements from Devil's Backbone had snagged her like a rusty fishhook in soft flesh.

Multiple survivors described the same impossible thing: a person who wasn't quite right, whose features shifted when you weren't looking directly at them, whose shadow moved independently of their body.

The locals called it the Hollow Man.

Joan adjusted her camera strap and checked her recording equipment one final time. She'd arranged to meet Tommy Bridwell, one of the few witnesses willing to talk, at the old mining camp that served as an unofficial trailhead. The rusted sign still bore the faded letters.

**DEVIL'S BACKBONE MINING CO. - EST. 1923 - CLOSED 1978**

Tommy was waiting by the abandoned equipment shed, a wiry man in his fifties whose hands shook constantly since his encounter three weeks ago. His eyes darted between the treeline and Joan's face, never settling on either for more than a few seconds.

"You sure you want to hear this, miss?" Tommy's voice carried the weight of sleepless nights. "Some things are better left buried in these hills."

Joan pulled out her digital recorder and set it on the weathered picnic table between them. "Tell me what you saw."

Tommy lit a cigarette with trembling fingers, the flame from his lighter casting dancing shadows across his weathered face. "I was bow hunting up on the ridge, maybe half a mile from Widow's Creek. Been hunting these woods for thirty years, know every deer path and rabbit run. That's when I saw him—or thought I did."

The older man took a long drag, the smoke mixing with the fog until Joan couldn't tell where one ended and the other began. "Looked like Jake

Morrison at first. You know Jake—runs the bait shop down in Russellville. Same height, same build, even wearing Jake's lucky hunting vest. But something was wrong with his face."

"Wrong how?"

"It kept... shifting. Like looking at your reflection in disturbed water. One second it was Jake's face, next it was someone else entirely. Then it turned to look at me, and I swear on my mother's grave, miss—it didn't have any eyes. Just smooth skin where they should've been, but I could feel it watching me anyway."

Joan's skin prickled with goosebumps that had nothing to do with the October chill. "What happened next?"

Tommy's cigarette had burned down to his fingers, but he didn't seem to notice. "It smiled. Not a human smile—too wide, too many teeth. Then it started walking toward me, and with each step, it changed. Jake's face melted away like candle wax, and underneath was something else. Something hungry."

"Did you see what it really looked like?"

"That's just it," Tommy whispered, his voice barely audible above the wind rustling through the dying leaves. "I don't think it has a real face. It's hollow inside, like its name says. Just wearing other people's skins like masks."

The interview continued for another twenty minutes, with Tommy describing his desperate flight through the woods and the inhuman howl that had followed him all the way back to his truck. By the time Joan packed up her equipment, the fog had thickened considerably, reducing visibility to maybe twenty feet in any direction.

"You're not thinking of going up there alone, are you?" Tommy asked as Joan shouldered her hiking pack.

"I'm a professional," she replied, though her voice carried less confidence than she intended. "I know how to take care of myself."

Tommy grabbed her arm as she turned toward the trailhead. His grip was surprisingly strong, and his eyes held a desperate intensity. "Listen to me, miss. That thing up there, it's not just a killer. It's a hunter. And it's been watching us this whole time."

Joan followed his gaze toward the treeline, where the fog seemed to swirl with unnatural purpose. For just a moment, she thought she saw a figure standing between the trees—tall, motionless, and somehow wrong in ways her brain refused to process. When she blinked, it was gone.

"I'll be careful," she said, gently pulling free from Tommy's grasp.

"Careful won't be enough," he called after her as she disappeared into the mist. "That thing doesn't just kill you. It takes your place."

The trail up Devil's Backbone Ridge was well-marked initially, but the deeper Joan hiked into the Ozark wilderness, the more the path seemed to fragment and fade. Ancient oak and hickory trees pressed close on either side, their branches forming a canopy so thick that the afternoon light barely penetrated to the forest floor. The fog moved between the trunks like something alive, occasionally parting to reveal glimpses of the rocky ridgeline above.

Joan had been hiking for nearly two hours when she found the first campsite. The orange tent was still standing, though one side had been slashed open with what looked like claws. Personal belongings were scattered across the small clearing—a sleeping bag torn to shreds, a camp stove overturned, and a backpack with its contents spilled across the dead leaves.

She approached carefully, pulling out her camera to document the scene. The registration tag attached to the tent's zipper identified the camper as Michael Vasquez from Little Rock. According to her research, he'd been reported missing six weeks ago after failing to return from a solo hiking trip.

That's when she noticed the blood.

It wasn't the rust-brown stain of old blood—this was fresh, crimson drops that led away from the campsite and deeper into the woods. Joan followed the trail with growing unease, her hiking boots squelching through patches of mud that seemed too red to be entirely earth and water.

# WHO GOES WHERE?

The blood trail ended at a massive oak tree whose trunk was easily eight feet in diameter. The bark had been carved with symbols that hurt to look at directly—angular marks that seemed to writhe and shift when caught in her peripheral vision. Nailed to the tree at eye level was something that made Joan's stomach lurch.

It was a face. Human skin stretched tight over some kind of frame, the features preserved with disturbing accuracy. The eyes were gone, but the mouth was frozen in a silent scream. A small placard beneath it bore the inscription.

## MICHAEL VASQUEZ - 10/15/2024

Joan stumbled backward, her camera nearly slipping from her trembling hands. As she raised it to take a photo, she noticed movement in her viewfinder. Someone was standing just at the edge of the frame, partially hidden behind another tree.

She lowered the camera and turned to look directly at the figure. It was a park ranger—or at least, someone wearing a ranger's uniform. Middle-aged, average build, with a face that seemed familiar though she was certain they'd never met.

"Ma'am, you shouldn't be up here alone," the ranger said, stepping into the clearing. His voice was professionally concerned but carried an odd echo, as if he were speaking from the bottom of a deep well. "These woods aren't safe right now."

"I'm documenting the disappearances for a story," Joan replied, trying to keep her voice steady. "Are you familiar with this... display?"

The ranger's eyes fixed on the grotesque trophy nailed to the oak. When he smiled, Joan noticed his teeth were too sharp and too numerous. "Oh yes, I'm very familiar with Michael's face. He had such interesting expressions before the end."

Joan's blood turned to ice water in her veins. The ranger was still smiling, but his features were beginning to blur and shift like heat waves rising from summer asphalt. The uniform sagged and stretched as the body underneath changed shape, becoming something taller and more angular.

"You know," the thing continued in a voice that was no longer quite human, "I've been wearing this ranger's skin for almost a month now. But it's getting a bit tight around the edges. I think it's time for something new."

Joan ran.

She crashed through the underbrush with no regard for stealth or direction, branches tearing at her jacket and face as she fled down the mountainside. Behind her, something was giving chase—not running exactly, but moving through the trees with fluid, inhuman grace. She could hear it laughing, a sound like wind through a graveyard.

A root caught her ankle, sending her tumbling down a steep embankment. She rolled through dead leaves and loose rocks, finally coming to rest in a small creek at the bottom of the hollow. The icy water shocked her back to her senses, and she struggled to her feet, looking around desperately for any sign of the trail.

The fog had grown so thick she could barely see her own hands. The creek gurgled around her boots, and somewhere in the mist, something was breathing heavily. Not like an animal—the rhythm was too deliberate, too patient.

"Joan," a voice called from the fog. It was her own voice, speaking her own name with perfect inflection. "Joan, where are you? I'm hurt."

The voice came from upstream, maybe thirty yards away. Joan pressed herself against a moss-covered boulder and tried to control her breathing. Whatever was hunting her had taken her voice, was using it to lure her closer.

"I fell down the embankment," her own voice continued, now with just the right note of pain and confusion. "I think my leg is broken. Please help me."

Joan bit her lip to keep from responding. The voice was so perfect, so convincing, that part of her actually wanted to go help herself. The shapeshifter had somehow captured not just her voice but the exact way she would sound if she were truly injured and afraid.

The breathing sound was getting closer. Joan could make out a dark shape moving through the fog, staying just at the edge of visibility. It was tall and thin, too thin, as if someone had stretched a human body like taffy. As it turned its head in her direction, she caught a glimpse of its face—or rather, the absence of one. Smooth skin stretched over an empty socket where features should have been.

"I know you're there, Joan," it said, still using her voice. "I can smell your fear. It smells like copper pennies and old flowers."

The thing began to change as it spoke. Its limbs shortened and filled out, taking on a more familiar shape. By the time it stepped fully into view, Joan was looking at herself—an exact duplicate down to the small scar on her chin from a childhood accident.

"This is much better," the duplicate said, running Joan's own hands over Joan's own face. "Young skin is so much more comfortable. And you have such interesting memories."

The shapeshifter's eyes—Joan's eyes—went completely black for a moment before returning to normal. "Oh, I see. You're writing a story about me. How delightfully meta. I'll make sure to give you a proper ending."

Joan waited until the thing turned away, then began moving carefully downstream. The creek bed was treacherous with smooth stones and hidden roots, but it offered the only clear path through the fog. She needed to get back to her car, needed to warn someone about what was loose in these woods.

She'd made it maybe a hundred yards when she heard her own voice calling again, this time from multiple directions. The shapeshifter was everywhere at once, or perhaps there was more than one of them. The voices overlapped and echoed through the hollow, creating a disorienting chorus of Joans all calling for help.

"Please," the voices pleaded. "I'm so scared. Don't leave me alone out here."

Joan forced herself to keep moving, following the creek as it wound deeper into the hollow. The fog began to thin slightly, and she could make out the rocky walls rising on either side. She was in a narrow canyon now, with steep cliffs that would be impossible to climb. The only way out was forward or back, and going back meant facing whatever was hunting her.

The creek made a sharp turn to the left, and Joan found herself in a wider area where the water pooled into a small pond. The surface was perfectly still, reflecting the gray sky above like a mirror. And floating face-down in the center of the pond was a park ranger's uniform, still occupied by something that had once been human.

The body was missing its face, the skull carved clean down to the bone. Chunks of flesh bobbed around it like grotesque lily pads. This was the real ranger, Joan realized—the one whose identity the shapeshifter had stolen.

"Beautiful work, isn't it?" The voice came from directly behind her. Joan spun around to find herself face-to-face with the thing wearing her skin. Up close, she could see the imperfections—the way the duplicate's smile was just a fraction too wide, the way its pupils dilated and contracted independently of the light.

"I've been practicing for so long," the Joan-thing continued, circling her like a predator. "First animals, then the occasional hiker. But humans are so much more complex. So many little details to get right."

"What are you?" Joan whispered.

The duplicate laughed, and for a moment its face rippled like water. "I'm whatever I need to be. But I suppose you could say I'm the original inhabitant of these hills. I was here long before the Cherokee, long before the miners, long before people like you came stomping through my territory with your cameras and your questions."

The shapeshifter's form began to change again, growing taller and more angular. Its skin took on a grayish tint, and when it opened its mouth, Joan could see rows of needle-sharp teeth.

"I've been sleeping in the deep caves for decades at a time, only waking when I get hungry. But lately, there's been so much food wandering into my domain. Hikers, hunters, campers—all so trusting, so eager to help a fellow human in distress."

Joan's hand closed around a sharp piece of shale that had fallen from the canyon wall. It wasn't much of a weapon, but it was better than nothing. "How many people have you killed?"

"Killed?" The thing seemed genuinely puzzled by the question. "I don't kill anyone, Joan. I become them. They live on through me, their memories and personalities preserved forever. In a way, I'm offering them immortality."

The shapeshifter lunged forward with inhuman speed, its fingers extending into claws that could have gutted a deer. Joan dove to the side, slashing with the piece of shale and opening a gash across the creature's arm. Instead of blood, a thick, dark fluid oozed from the wound.

The thing hissed in pain and anger, its perfect Joan-face contorting into something monstrous. "You little bitch! Do you have any idea how long it takes to properly integrate a new identity?"

Joan scrambled up the rocky slope beside the pond, her boots slipping on the wet stone. Behind her, the shapeshifter was changing again, its limbs stretching and twisting into something that could climb the sheer rock face with ease.

She reached a narrow ledge about twenty feet above the water and pressed herself against the canyon wall. The creature followed, moving up the rock face like a spider, its fingers finding impossible handholds in the solid stone.

"There's nowhere to run, Joan," it called up to her. "And really, why would you want to? I'll take such good care of your identity. Your family will never know the difference. Your friends will think you've simply moved away to pursue new opportunities. I'll live your life better than you ever could."

The shapeshifter reached the ledge and hauled itself up with fluid grace. This close, Joan could see that its eyes were completely solid black now, like pools of crude oil. When it smiled, its teeth had multiplied into rows like a shark's.

"I've been studying you since you arrived," it continued, advancing across the narrow ledge. "Reading your memories as I slowly take on your form. Did you know you still dream about your college boyfriend? Marcus, wasn't it? The one who died in the car accident?"

Joan's grip tightened on the piece of shale. "Stay out of my head."

"Too late for that, I'm afraid. I'm already inside, sorting through your experiences like files in a cabinet. Your first kiss, your worst nightmare, the way you cried when your father left—it's all mine now."

The creature reached out with one elongated arm, its fingers brushing against Joan's cheek in a mockery of tenderness. "I'll make sure to visit your mother for you. She's been so worried since you moved to Chicago. I'll tell her you're doing well, that you've found peace in these beautiful mountains."

Joan struck without warning, driving the sharp edge of the shale deep into the shapeshifter's throat. The creature stumbled backward, that dark fluid pouring from the wound and sizzling where it hit the stone.

For a moment, its stolen face flickered through a dozen different identities—the park ranger, various hikers, even what might have been its original form, something pale and eyeless and absolutely inhuman. Then it stabilized back into Joan's appearance, though now with a gaping wound across its neck.

"Clever girl," it gurgled, its voice distorted by the injury. "But you can't kill something that was never truly alive."

The wound began to close, the edges of flesh knitting together with disturbing speed. Within seconds, the shapeshifter's throat was whole again, though its skin had taken on a more pronounced grayish pallor.

Joan backed away along the ledge, searching desperately for another escape route. The ledge curved around the canyon wall, possibly leading to another way down. She just had to stay ahead of the creature long enough to find it.

But the shapeshifter had other plans. It suddenly launched itself forward, not trying to grab her but simply to knock her off balance. Joan

# WHO GOES WHERE?

felt her feet slip on the damp stone, and then she was falling backward through empty air.

She hit the pond with a tremendous splash, the icy water closing over her head like a fist. For a moment she was disoriented, not sure which way was up, her lungs burning with the need for air. Then she broke the surface, gasping and thrashing, trying to keep her head above water.

The pond was deeper than it looked, and the bottom was thick with decades of accumulated mud and decomposing organic matter. As Joan struggled to stay afloat, her hand brushed against something soft and yielding beneath the water. She looked down and screamed.

There were bodies down there—dozens of them in various states of decay. Some were recent enough to still have faces, their empty eye sockets staring up at her through the murky water. Others were little more than skeletons held together by rotting tendons. And floating among them were the faces the shapeshifter had collected, dozens of human masks preserved in the cold water like grotesque lily pads.

Joan kicked frantically toward the shore, but the mud at the bottom of the pond seemed to be pulling at her boots. Something grabbed her ankle—a skeletal hand attached to the remains of what had once been a person. More hands reached up from the depths, the shapeshifter's previous victims trying to drag her down to join them in their eternal rest.

"My children want to meet you," the creature called from the ledge above. It was crouched at the edge like a gargoyle, watching her struggle with evident amusement. "They've been so lonely down there in the cold and dark."

Joan managed to break free from the grasping hands and make it to the shallows, crawling up onto a muddy bank on the far side of the pond. Her clothes were soaked and heavy, and her skin felt like ice, but she was alive.

The shapeshifter dropped from the ledge with predatory grace, landing on the rocks beside the water without making a sound. "You're beginning to irritate me, Joan. I was hoping we could do this the easy way—a quick transformation, minimal suffering. But you insist on making it difficult."

The creature began to change again, its human disguise melting away like candle wax. What emerged was something that had never been human, something that belonged in the deepest caves beneath the mountains. It stood nearly eight feet tall on legs that bent in too many places, its skin the color of old bones. Its face was a smooth expanse of flesh punctuated only by a mouth filled with concentric rows of teeth.

"This is what I really am," it said, its voice now a wet whisper that seemed to come from everywhere at once. "I am the thing that waits in the dark places, the hunger that can never be satisfied. I have worn a thousand faces and lived a thousand lives, but I am always, eternally empty inside."

Joan backed away from the water's edge, looking for anything she could use as a weapon. The canyon walls were too steep to climb, and the only way out was past the creature. She was trapped.

But then she noticed something the shapeshifter had missed in its transformation. The faces floating in the pond were moving, drifting toward the shore where the creature stood. And they weren't alone—skeletal hands were emerging from the water, followed by the shambling forms of the shapeshifter's victims.

"What—" the creature began, then turned to see its previous prey rising from their watery grave. The dead moved with purpose, their empty eye sockets fixed on their killer with unmistakable hunger.

"Impossible," the shapeshifter hissed. "You're mine. I consumed you, took your identities, made you part of me."

But the dead weren't listening. They surrounded the creature in a circle of rotting flesh and exposed bone, their movements coordinated despite their individual decay.

The shapeshifter lashed out with its claws, tearing through several of the walking corpses, but more kept coming. They grabbed at its arms and legs with their bony fingers, dragging it toward the pond. The creature's inhuman strength allowed it to throw them off initially, but there were simply too many of them.

"No!" it screamed as they pulled it into the water. "I am eternal! I am the hunger that devours all!"

The pond began to boil with activity as the dead dragged their killer down into the depths. Joan watched in horrified fascination as the shapeshifter's form shifted frantically through dozens of stolen identities, trying to find one that could escape this fate. But the dead remembered every face it had worn, every life it had stolen, and they wanted their justice.

The last thing Joan saw before the water went still was the creature's original face—pale, eyeless, and utterly alien—disappearing beneath the surface with a gurgling scream.

For several minutes, the pond remained active with bubbles and strange movements beneath the surface. Gradually, everything went quiet. The bodies of the dead sank back to the bottom, their moment of vengeance complete. The stolen faces dissolved like mist, finally freed from their preservation.

Joan stood alone in the canyon, shivering in her wet clothes and trying to process what she'd witnessed. The fog was beginning to lift, and she could see a narrow path leading up the far wall of the canyon—a way out that hadn't been visible before.

As she climbed toward daylight and safety, Joan made a mental note to burn her story notes when she got home. Some things were too dangerous to share with the world, too terrible to risk someone else coming to investigate. The Hollow Man was gone, dragged down by its victims to whatever hell awaited creatures like it.

But as she reached the top of the canyon and looked back at the still pond below, Joan couldn't shake the feeling that something was watching her go. The shapeshifter had claimed to be eternal, after all. And in the deep caves beneath the Ozark Mountains, there might be others like it, waiting for their turn to wake and hunt.

She walked faster, eager to put as much distance as possible between herself and Devil's Backbone Ridge. Behind her, the fog rolled back in, swallowing the canyon and its secrets once more.

Deep beneath the water, something stirred in the mud, patient and hungry and very much alive.

The drive back to Chicago took fourteen hours, but Joan barely stopped except for gas. Every time she closed her eyes, she saw that terrible, eyeless face rising from the pond, its mouth full of too many teeth. She'd gotten her story, but it was one she'd never be able to tell.

Three weeks later, she read about a park ranger who'd gone missing from the Devil's Backbone area. The description matched the man whose uniform she'd seen floating in the pond, whose identity the shapeshifter had stolen. The search teams found no trace of him, just like all the others.

Joan deleted the photos from her camera and threw away her notes. She never wrote about the Ozarks again. But sometimes, late at night when the fog rolled through the Chicago streets, she'd catch a glimpse of a familiar face in her peripheral vision—her own face, watching her from the shadows with eyes like pools of crude oil.

The thing in the pond wasn't dead. It was waiting. And sooner or later, it would remember how good she tasted, how perfectly she'd fit into its collection of stolen lives.

Joan moved to Arizona six months later, as far from the mountains as she could get. But she knew it wouldn't matter. Some hungers are patient, and the thing that wore faces like masks had learned to wait.

In the deep caves beneath Devil's Backbone Ridge, something stirred in its sleep and smiled with a mouth full of stolen teeth. It had tasted Joan Lamont's memories, savored her fears, and it would find her again when the time was right. After all, it was eternal, and it was always, always hungry.

The fog rolled through the Ozark hollows, carrying the scent of old bones and older evils.

Somewhere in the mist, the Hollow Man began to walk again.

# SONGBIRD LANE

## TROY SEATE

Robert had begun to lock up when the phone rang. He looked at the instrument as if it were some alien creature determined to interfere with his life. It was six o'clock and pitch-black outside. A frigid evening wrapped itself around his world. The roads were icing over and he had eleven miles to drive. He didn't want to answer, but he did.

"Citizens," he said hurriedly.

*Whispering voices and scratching sounds.*

The connection broke off with a soft click. The room suddenly seemed as cavernous and foreboding as an empty mortuary. Robert returned the phone to its cradle and turned everything off save the lights that burned all night.

Outside, ice crystals swirled around him as he made haste from the bank's rear door to his Civic. The cold turned his breath into milky plumes.

Robert climbed into the car, the heat from inside the building quickly seeping away. At least his vehicle could be counted on to fire up even in the coldest weather and navigate the Ozarks' hills and hollers.

The ignition caught. He let the engine warm before engaging the heat and backing out of his spot. After dark the streets looked ugly and alien. They were also deserted, making the last signal light out of the little mountain town seem extravagant.

A car hadn't passed the bank in the last fifteen minutes, so there would be mercifully little traffic. Several blocks beyond the bank and the traffic light, he turned onto Songbird Lane without incident.

He'd heard all the supernatural nonsense about this ten-mile stretch. Small towns as country as Conway Twitty loved their legends as much as the preserves they put up in glass jars, so the stories about Songbird played well.

He and his wife had purchased a nice-sized fixer-upper along the infamous route. Ghostly legends or not, it was a deal too good to pass up. It complemented his decision to take the banking job and leave the hustle and bustle of city life behind.

At this moment, however, his decision was not comforting. His automobile's heat wasn't putting out as it should. Robert grumbled and messed with the dials as he drove. What he didn't need was a trip to the dealer two counties away.

He concentrated on the two-way stretch of blacktop with its rises and falls and curves, mindful of ice. He was a good driver. No accidents, no citations, but the countryside's winding roads could make anyone a novice. Nasty weather was treacherous, but at a steady thirty miles per hour, he'd be home in close to twenty minutes.

With his eyes focused on the road's midline, he thought about hearth and home, the warm kitchen with Marilyn preparing a hot meal, the girls either arguing or playing contentedly depending on how their day had gone. Had he made a mistake by dragging them to a rural location and a house with some renovations yet to be tackled? Marilyn had been a good sport even while encountering unreliable gas and water pipes.

Robert's mind wandered to the universal legend of the unwanted passenger, symbolic of all the formless imaginings of danger and terror.

*A woman stops to get gas. After paying inside, another motorist yells something as she returns to her car. She quickly climbs in and drives away. The man starts his engine and pursues her. On the radio, the woman hears about a maniac loose in the area. Her breath catches in her chest, scared to death her pursuer is the ballyhooed maniac in a stolen vehicle.*

*The road is slick and winding. Her tires slide sideways, sending the car off the road into a ditch. Shaken but uninjured, she sees the other car stop. She jumps out and runs. A house looms nearby. She rushes up the steps and frantically pounds on the door until the homeowner opens up.*

*"A man's after me. He's trying to kill me," she cries.*

*The motorist from the trailing car runs to the house as the woman cringes behind the homeowner. "Thank God you got out of the car, lady," her pursuer says. "When you went inside the station, a man climbed into your backseat."*

End of story.

A slight grin split Robert's face. Interesting how a lonely road like this one could capture one's thoughts. Songbird Lane whoppers included a ghost boy by a bridge, Satan worshippers behind trees, and other sundry myths. He found these fanciful tales preferable to the prospect of a real event such as the backseat story, but either way, this dark path could tap into one's innermost fears.

"Pay attention to your driving, city-boy," he murmured.

In spite of his care, one of his tires found a pothole four miles into the journey, causing the Civic to veer into the oncoming lane. *No traffic, thank God.*

Robert drove on, pondering the damage an icy slide could cause. Running off the road's soft shoulder and into a tree wasn't the way to end a long, tedious day.

He pushed a button to turn on the radio. He couldn't even raise a good ole country knee-snapper. Nothing but static. He began to worry about the vehicle's entire electrical system as he gripped the steering wheel a little tighter, his hands at ten and two o'clock, and strained to watch the road more carefully.

He guided the Civic dead center down the dividing line. The world on either side of the road seemed surreal, a deserted, desolate place, an icicle world from a fairy tale. The only reality was his vehicle and the part of the road caught in the headlight beams.

The strange phone call. Was that the reason for his growing uneasiness?

*Not far to go.*

Headlights appeared in the distance. He wasn't alone with the lane's potholes after all. As the vehicle approached, Robert could tell it was going much too fast for the conditions. Its bright lights made his eyes squint. He slowed and pulled as close to the outer edge of the shoulder as he dared.

Goosebumps pebbled his flesh as the vehicle blew by him at an unsafe speed—a big black monstrosity. The Civic shook from its force. A miscalculation could have quickly turned Robert and his car into an unattractive burgundy waffle.

"Damned idiot," Robert groused. He returned to a steady pace of only twenty-five miles per hour. Better safe than sorry, but the encounter had shaken him. The heater was still blowing cold.

A touch of tingling disquiet climbed his spine. "Only about five more miles," he said aloud, but his sense of urgency was growing. He tried to focus on his family and the warm kitchen where they would eat and talk and then drift off to their respective smart phones.

He was over halfway home when another pair of headlights appeared in his rearview. This vehicle approached just as rapidly as the last one.

"What's with these local yokels?" he pondered. Granted, they might understand the road conditions better than he, but who had ever heard of the people around here being in a hurry? They sure weren't in a hurry when it came to paying their mortgages.

Robert and Marilyn reasoned their move would provide a more idyllic lifestyle where his two daughters could breathe fresh air and his family could feel a little safer than in the city. That cut little ice at the moment as he considered the approaching headlights. He found the edge of the pavement again and gave the crazy driver as much room to pass as possible.

The vehicle roared up to within a car length, then held its speed and trailed him. Robert slowed even more. If it hadn't been so cold, he would have lowered his window and waved for the vehicle to pass, but eventually, it sped from behind and quickly swept up alongside the Civic.

Robert glanced over. It was large—a tank of a car. He could sense the heft of it beside him. *Too big for the icy curves.* Illumination from the dash played on the driver, whose head turned in Robert's direction as if on a swivel. It was a chilling sight. There was an antique look about him, like a figure out of a wax museum, no one he knew from town or from bank business.

As Robert stared, the vehicle soon gathered speed and streaked past, inserting itself on the road in front of the Civic. Robert's headlights revealed strange things about the black sedan. It had no plates or distinguishing marks. It resembled the vehicle that had passed him earlier.

It looked a lot like a... he hesitated to even think about it. *A hearse,* not the kind of vehicle you expected to run across in the dark... in the night... on a slippery Ozark road.

The Civic windshield took on a barrage of ice slivers from the lead car's rear tires. Robert's wipers fought the sludge for a few seconds before the car zoomed ahead, its taillights glowing like two red eyes. It rapidly disappeared into the darkness as if the driver thought he was immortal, safe at any speed.

Conditions were deteriorating. Robert cautiously held his speed to twenty-five. Just another four miles, give or take. He tried to imagine the smells coming from their kitchen and the way Marilyn would smile at him when he trudged in from the garage.

But then something more challenged his senses. No sooner had the taillights ahead winked out than the same car appeared once again to his left like a black hulking ghost. Robert had never believed in coincidence, had never trusted fate. His heart leaped into his throat. *It can't be.*

The vehicle recklessly swung into the lane in front of him, missing the Civic by only a few inches and causing another spray on the windshield. The Civic's outside wheels hit the shoulder. Robert strained to hold the vehicle on course.

*He's trying to kill me.*

Robert had never experienced terror but quickly found that it could shove aside logic in a heartbeat provoking a needle-sharp stinging in the base of the skull. This joker was either into mindless aggression or had been made stupid by drink.

He suddenly remembered another legend about a phantom driver, the piece of folklore that provided the biggest laugh at the bank party in his honor when his family moved to the area.

"Enough of this," he said loudly, in need of a reasonable explanation. The driver was clearly nuts, traveling so fast at night on an icy road.

But the paradox persisted. *The same long, black car with the frightening silhouetted driver.* Philosophical questions about being singled out for ruin by a murderous crazy would have to wait. He just wanted to get home and off the road.

He slowly pulled off altogether and stopped the car as the taillights ahead disappeared once more. The way his night was going, he couldn't keep from twisting around and looking into the well behind the front seat. A nutcase lying in wait would have been more acceptable than some mysterious road warrior with a death wish.

Robert fished his phone from his jacket and pushed buttons. It started to ring. He heard the click registering a connection. There was no "Hello." Just static at first, then voices whispering, sounding unearthly, the same sounds from the telephone at work.

"Natalie? Jenny? If it's either one of you, please put your mother on."

A giggle preceded a disconnect. The small screen went dark and the acute silence lasted for several heartbeats. He hadn't realized how truly frightened he was until he heard the sounds coming from his own house. *The girls weren't ones to screw around with the phone and why hadn't Marilyn answered?*

Fighting off panic, Robert put the Civic back in drive and pulled off the shoulder, feeling the need to get home ASAP. *Not much farther to go.* He was no longer concerned about the ice build-up or the other vehicle. He was only interested in the safety of his family.

The car churned out a little heat, but Robert remained as cold as the night air, a chill which ran into the recesses of his mind as well as his body. Something sinister was happening to a rational man who spent his time managing details with numbers and balance sheets.

One last hurdle before reaching the driveway to his front porch—a narrow bridge over a deep ravine. It was known to be especially treacherous on evenings such as this. A speed limit sign warned drivers to slow to twenty miles per hour when crossing, even in good weather. He thought about ringing his house again but wanted all his attention on navigating the last mile.

A hungry darkness lay on either side of the road. Everything had become unfamiliar. Reality had turned into a mysterious shadowland steeped with evil. The headlamps lit peripheral fence posts and cast surreal, grotesque, shifting shadows along the route like brooding gods from another world prowling the night.

Occasional tree phantoms shaped all the monsters of myth. They clawed out from both sides of the blacktop now covered with a whiteness representing something less than purity. In spite of the cold, a bead of sweat trickled from Robert's temple down to his jaw.

The penchant for numerical analyses pushed his accountant's mind into overdrive. Maybe it wasn't the black vehicle at all. Maybe it was the road itself—*Songbird Lane*. What an innocent moniker for this dangerous ribbon of pavement. Maybe an evil force ran under it like an aquifer he'd somehow tapped in to. Maybe the horrific legends had purchase in the cold of night.

Was he hostage to a nightmare? The vehicle passing him again—wasn't it like the nightmare about running but getting nowhere, or the one where something is whispered about and is known by everyone but you?

He imagined unpleasant things leaping out in front of his Civic, or sudden thumps on its roof top, his thoughts bordering on hysteria. Fear was one of the reasons they had left the city. Danger felt out of place on the road with the pleasant, melodic name… until now.

Yet here it was, fear clinging to the banker. The journey's events had planted the specter of a nervous breakdown.

Though the night closed in like a tunnel, the bridge was now in reach of the headlights, its railing on either side reminding Robert of two rows of teeth. "Almost there. Just like *Sleepy Hollow's* Ichabod Crane. Make it to the far side of the bridge and to safety. I'll slow—"

On the far side of the bridge sat an ominous pair of headlights. Robert held his breath. An awful, sick feeling sunk into his marrow. This was to be more than a game of chicken or insane recklessness. It wasn't imagination or paranoia. The car was there… waiting.

He thought: *I'll close my eyes and all of this will disappear*.

He thought: *I've fallen asleep in the office and am having a nightmare*.

He thought: *No, I'm still here on this accursed night*.

He thought: *And for whatever reason, the person driving the phantom seeks to destroy me*.

Another emotion grabbed hold.

*Loneliness*.

Would he ever see his family again? What would they do without him? What would he do without *them*?

The countryside was now no more than a blur, the road all that was left of the world. Robert started across the bridge, but by the time he'd driven a third of the way, the black vehicle started across at the other end and bore down on him at high speed. There was no turning back. No chance to back up or let the demon car pass. If he swerved to the right or left, he'd be through the guardrail and into the ravine.

Onward the maniac came, right down the middle of Songbird Lane, racing straight at the Civic. The black car was doing sixty to Robert's twenty. The momentum would carry the cars into a collision no matter what, he'd be smashed like a pancake. Still, Robert had to do *something*. His life was reduced to the question of: should he drive off the bridge or keep going straight?

From some remote pocket in Robert's mind, he remembered a saying he'd once heard. *If the devil comes a knockin', don't turn your back on him. Go toe to toe.*

No time for hesitation.

Robert put his foot to the accelerator. Adrenaline rushed through him like a blue flame as the two sets of headlights approached one another. A second before impact, Robert braced his arms and closed his eyes. In that split second, he wondered if his life would flash before his eyes.

Then he started to scream.

A horrific *swooshing* sound went past him—through him, like a jolt of electricity. He opened his eyes and hit the brakes. The Civic skidded and slid to a slippery halt. He relaxed his grip on the wheel. He was safely on the far side of the bridge. The hearse-like demon-car had been no more than a phantom after all.

Melancholy came over him. Fatigue replaced tension and Robert was no longer cold. *But why all of this otherworldly theatrics?* He felt on the edge of an alternate dimension, as if eyes on the other side were watching him. Exhaling a relieved sigh, he continued the final distance to his house. He could begin to feel the warmth of it even now.

The sky had cleared. Robert could see the stars wheeling in the darkness. As he turned the final bend on Songbird Lane, past a copse of dark, bare trunks and limbs, another surprise awaited. Robert stared across a snow-covered field.

The glow in the distance was not the lingering rays from a departed sun, or the teasing pallet of pastels signaling a reluctant dawn. It was something else: yellow-orange tongues of flame.

Within ten yards of the turnoff to his driveway, he slammed his foot against the brake pedal once again. He pushed himself against the driver's door but couldn't get it to open.

A firetruck, moving much too slowly, was rolling down the road from the opposite direction. It pulled into Robert's drive, blue and red lights flashing through the freezing night. Smoke and crackling bursts of flames belched from every window and door of his house, reaching into the sky, beauty and horror inescapably twined together.

A quiet serenity overtook him. Why didn't he feel crazy with dread about the welfare of Marilyn and the girls? Losing loved ones in such a horrific way from a leaky gas pipe, more than likely. Human beings weren't built to withstand this kind of hurt. Why wasn't he out of his mind with grief, overcome by the suffocating weight of despair at the possibility of his family trapped inside an inferno and burning to death, their home becoming a funeral pyre? Phantom echoes of dying screams should have assaulted him.

The answer was coming in his direction. The long vehicle trailed behind the firetruck and a patrol car rolling up the drive to Robert's burning house. Instead of turning with the other two vehicles, the transport rolled down the ten yards of icy road toward the Civic. It passed Robert, but this time, it traveled slowly.

He could see inside the black sedan now. In the front passenger seat sat his wife, Marilyn, beside the lanky, pasty-faced driver. In the back sat Natalie and Jenny, his daughters. For Robert, it hadn't been necessary to stare into the abyss and travel the stages of shock and denial. When the vehicle passed by, he understood everything.

*Creator, destroyer. He gives, He takes away.*

He knew where the vehicle was going this time. It was traveling to the icy bridge on Songbird Lane to pick up another passenger. The moonlight pointed a pale finger back to a spot near the bridge and he could now see his burgundy Civic as it truly was.

It had careened off into the gully. It rested in a heap, its front end totally demolished. Parts of a person were in the front seat behind the engine block which had been shoved through the firewall and now rested in front of the figure as if being cradled.

But the smashed figure wasn't *him*. It wasn't Robert Hoskins. Because Robert was waiting by the road to be picked up by the phantom driver. If his family was leaving, *his* remaining behind would have been like some cosmic, clerical error. He would have been left with the condolences of well-meaning people and a new kind of isolation with only his family's memory etched on his soul. He wouldn't have wanted that.

The loneliness had lifted. There was just enough room for one more traveler next to his two daughters in the back seat. They wouldn't be on the treacherous Songbird Lane much longer.

And Robert didn't have to worry about macabre voices on the phone or demons any longer, or the bank, or the wisdom of their move, or about legends, real or imaginary.

Sooner or later, the universe was about balance like his spreadsheets. Planets would align. Everything was settled now as he'd been given the opportunity to join his family on their journey to whatever destination they were headed to, leaving one more story to grace the Ozarks' and Songbird Lane's folklore.

# SPEAK, THAT THE FLAME MAY SLEEP

## ZARY FEKETE

**The Riders**
*They once roamed this land. Circuit Riders. Preachers in thin coats with worn Bibles. That time is long gone now. Some say it's because of the railway making obsolete the horse and hoof. But there are other rumors…*

*Sit down here with me. I have a story to tell.*

My horse had begun to lather at his shoulders. Poor thing. Steam and breath came from him in short bursts, and he stumbled as his hooves sparked on the rocky path. I gripped the rein, wiping my eyes and peering into the fog that had enveloped our trail since morning. The earth climbed below us, not steep, but steady, and the air had started to smart on my knuckles like when the clouds are close to sleeting.

Ahead of me, the Reverend did not slow.

His frame was tall in the saddle, his face lost in shadow from the wide-brimmed hat he always wore on the trail, but I didn't need to see the face to know what was there. It was always the same when he rode: jaw set, mouth a grim line, tongue in his mouth working, as though he were reciting back scripture to himself.

He never spoke on the road—said words were like coins, if you spent them before you reached the destination you wouldn't have nothing left for the offering.

This had been his circuit for twenty-six years. It held five towns, eight outposts, and two chapels by forgotten cemeteries whose graves had swallowed up the villages that used to be there.

It was his job to preach, and he preached in every place. Whether they showed up or not.

I was his student even though he never used that word. The orphanage I came from had few options for when a child aged out at eighteen. Most boys went to the mines. The girls hoped for jobs as maids and scullery workers.

A few, like me, were scooped up by the church. The Reverend nodded once when I was introduced to him by the orphanage master. He asked if I could ride, and when I said yes, he replied, "Then you can serve the road as I have."

We had left Crosshollow at dawn and hadn't seen a soul since midday. Now the trail had narrowed to a single path between pines, and the mist grew thicker with each turn. Somewhere below us, a stream sang under the rocks, but the trees muffled the sound until it was more memory than music.

Then, just as the last light was draining out of the sky, I saw it.

The chapel.

It stood alone on a bald patch of ridge, its steeple leaning slightly eastward like it was bowing into the wind. The wood was gray with age, the roof missing slates. A single stained-glass window above the door flickered with orange, the first sign of firelight we'd seen in hours.

The Reverend dismounted without a word. I followed suit, my legs stiff from the ride. My boots crunched on frost-hardened grass. The cold here was different. Not a windchill kind of cold. A deep, dry cold that seemed to reach up through the soles of your feet and settle behind your ribs.

The chapel door creaked open before we reached it.

No one stood in the doorway.

No wind pushed it.

It simply opened.

The Reverend tipped his hat to the empty frame. "The Word goes where it's sent," he said, and stepped inside.

I hesitated, just a moment, watching that open doorway.

Then I followed.

## The Preaching

The inside of the chapel smelled of cedar and ash. A narrow iron stove hissed in the corner, its pipe rattling softly from the draw. The pews—twelve of them, six to a side—were bowed in the middle from years of bodies bending forward, waiting for words that might save or damn them. The pulpit was nothing more than a box nailed to the floorboards, but it was smooth with polish, worn to a soft sheen where countless palms had rested.

There were no candles. No hymnals. Just the glow of firelight, and above the altar, carved directly into the wood paneling, the words:

THE WORD IS A SWORD. SPEAK WITH BLOOD.

The Reverend removed his hat and hung it on the wall peg by the door. He knelt at the altar, silent. I sat on the back pew, unsure of what was expected. The stillness pressed in like a stifling blanket.

After a while, he stood.

"Rest," he said. "They'll come."

He was right.

By morning, they were there.

Quietly, singly, in pairs. Mostly older men, faces lined like maps, boots caked with the red dirt of the hills. A woman with a child on her hip. A boy of maybe twelve, carrying a sack of apples. They didn't greet each other. They just filed in and sat. Their eyes flicked toward the pulpit, then down to their hands. One woman crossed herself, even though this wasn't that kind of chapel.

When the last of them had settled, the Reverend stepped up to the front.

He opened the Bible—not his, but the chapel's, a massive volume kept chained to the stand. The chain clinked as he turned the pages. Then he laid one hand flat across the parchment and looked up.

There was no greeting. No announcements. No songs.

He simply began.

"The burden of sin is not seen with mortal eyes," he said. His voice was low, steady, but it carried. "It is not weighed like stone, nor poured like grain. But it gathers just the same."

No one moved.

He turned another page.

"Some burdens break the back. But sin... sin breaks the soul, and you don't feel it until you reach for water and find your hand full of dust."

A whisper passed through the room. Not words. Just the sound of people shifting, breathing.

The Reverend closed the Bible, but spoke on, the words clearly embedded in his mind.

"You who walk with secrets in your pockets. You who bury them beneath your porch stones. He sees. He counts. He waits."

The woman with the child began to cry. Not loudly. Just a soft, leaking sound. The boy next to her clutched her arm.

"Do not mistake His patience for absence," the Reverend said. "He is not late. He is exact. And He is nearer than your next thought."

His voice began to rise—not yelling, not yet, but with heat.

"The ridge remembers."

I blinked. That wasn't scripture. Not any that I knew.

"This very ground has soaked with sin like cloth with oil. And fire waits only for the right breath to catch it."

The old man in the third pew let out a single, rasping cough. But he didn't stand. No one did. They all stayed and took it.

The Reverend's hands clenched the pulpit.

"You are dry timber in a holy wind. Repent."

And then he fell silent.

A long pause.

No benediction. No closing prayer.

He stepped down and walked past the pews without looking at anyone. I stood quickly and followed him out into the cold. When we reached the horses, I asked him what I thought was a simple question.

"Did you mean to say that part about the ridge remembering?"

He looked at me for a long moment, the kind that makes you feel like you've already said too much.

"Remember your question," he said. "Sometimes the answers present themselves when you ride."

Then he mounted, and we rode on.

**The House with No Cross**

We didn't stop for lunch.

The Reverend said little as we rode. His mare moved with certainty, as if she knew the path better than he did. The trail narrowed again, shouldered in by pine and birch, and the mist that had lifted for the sermon returned, thicker now, clinging low to the ground like something alive.

I tried to shake the feeling that had settled over me after the chapel. It was the silence, I told myself. Too long. Too clean. Like the forest had been listening, and now it needed time to think.

It was near dusk when he pulled his horse up short and raised one hand.

"There," he said.

I followed his gaze. Just ahead, half-buried in snowmelt and shadow, was a house, barely more than a shack. The boards had gone silver with age, and the roof sagged in the middle. A chimney leaned crooked at one end. The windows were dark.

There was no cross on the door.

No sign of blessing. No charm. No pine bough. Not even a horseshoe nailed over the lintel.

"This is the one," he said.

"The one what?" I asked.

He dismounted. "The house where the Word hasn't walked."

As he approached the door, it opened. Not all at once, but slow, like someone didn't want to be seen doing it.

A young woman stood there.

She looked maybe seventeen. Barefoot. Her dress was thin, her hair tied back in a loose braid. Her face was white, not with sickness but with something like fear. Her eyes found mine, for just a moment, and in that second, I saw something I didn't want to name.

She looked at the Reverend, and then—quietly, like someone surrendering—she stepped aside to let him in.

He didn't look back at me. The door shut behind him. But before it did, something moved in the darkness within. It was large.

I stayed where I was. My hands clenched the reins tight.

It was fully dark now, except for a single line of orange firelight slipping between the bottom of the door and the warped floorboards.

Then I heard it.

Not talking.

Not a struggle.

But a sound with rhythm.
A wet, snapping crack.
Then a pause.
Then again.
Again.

The sound of a belt or a switch against skin. Muffled gasps between. And then… hisses.

I slid from the saddle but didn't move forward. I couldn't. My legs locked up.

Inside, another blow landed. Then silence.

The door opened.

The Reverend stepped out, adjusting his coat sleeves. His face was sweating. He took deep breaths, the actions of a man who had run a long course.

He didn't say anything for a moment. He just looked off into the trees. I could hear the faint trickle of a creek somewhere beyond the ridge.

"The darkness had settled deep," he said finally.

I stared at him.

"She'll sleep now," he said. "And when she wakes, she'll be clean."

He mounted his mare and looked down at me. "Some houses," he said, "you don't preach to from a pulpit. Some doors open only to the rod."

He turned the horse and began to ride.

I stood there a moment longer, listening. But the shack was silent again.

Then I followed.

## The Confession

We rode until near midnight.

Neither of us spoke.

The trail turned jagged after the last ridge. Stones jutted from the earth like broken teeth, and every few yards one of the horses stumbled, shaking its head as though something unseen was clinging to its ears. Above us, the moon hung behind clouds, offering light but no comfort.

Eventually, we made camp beneath a stand of spruce, their roots braided deep through the frost-hardened soil. The Reverend built a fire with practiced hands. I unrolled my bedroll and sat down, the chill still in my bones.

He said grace before eating, as he always did… slow, measured, like he was speaking not to God but to someone sitting just outside the circle of firelight.

Afterward, he lay down and folded his arms over his chest.

He fell asleep fast.

But sleep did not come to me.

I watched him. Watched the firelight flicker against his face, carving shadows deep into the folds of his skin. His lips moved, almost imperceptibly. I leaned closer, thinking he was praying.

But it wasn't prayer.

It was whispering.

Low. Broken.

I heard phrases… some from Scripture, others... wrong.

*"The blood shall cleanse..."*

*"The wilderness makes no promises..."*

*"She asked for the rod. She did. She did."*

I sat back. The skin along my arms was prickled, my breath shallow.

I reached into my pack for the small leather Bible I carried. I hadn't opened it in days. I wasn't sure why.

The cover felt colder than it should have.

I opened it to the first page.

Something was wrong.

The names were wrong.

Where it should have said *Matthew*, it said *Matron*. The Beatitudes were garbled, half of them rewritten in unfamiliar phrasing:

*Blessed are the silent, for they shall not be heard.*

*Blessed are the watchers, for they see the thing behind the veil.*

I flipped faster. *John* was there, but it wasn't the gospel I knew. It had verses I'd never read before. Things that didn't feel like misprints… they felt older. Hungrier.

I shut the book and held it in my lap, my heart pounding.

The fire crackled once, sharp and sudden.

The Reverend opened his eyes.

"Reading?" he asked.

I didn't answer.

He sat up slowly, as though waking from something heavier than sleep.

"The Word is alive," he said. "It speaks. Sometimes it speaks back."

I forced my voice to stay level. "My Bible has... errors."

He nodded, like that was no surprise at all.

"The Word isn't paper," he said. "It's not ink. The page is only what the Word wears, like skin. It can change its clothes."

I stared at him.

He stood and walked to the edge of the firelight.

"The circuit doesn't just go over hills and towns," he said. "It loops through time. Through sorrow. Through judgment. Each ride changes the rider."

He looked back at me.

"Some things you can only learn once you've carried the Word long enough."

He let that sit. Then he lay back down. And this time, when he whispered, I didn't lean in. I turned away and watched the trees.

Somewhere in the dark, an owl called once.

But no wind blew.

And sleep, when it came, was thin and fevered and full of hollow-eyed figures standing at doorways with mouths full of fire.

## The Final Circuit

The last chapel stood at the edge of the world.

We reached it by a trail so narrow we had to dismount and lead the horses single-file. The trees here leaned away from the clearing, their roots half-exposed, as though trying to escape. The air was brittle, sour with iron and smoke, though no fire burned. Beneath the smell was something worse… mildew and marrow and something like wet hair.

The chapel squatted low, roof slumped like a beast at rest. No windows. No cross. Only a ring of black earth where nothing grew.

The Reverend didn't hesitate. He walked straight to the door and placed his hand on the wood.

"She's been quiet," he said. "But quiet's not the same as gone."

I didn't ask what he meant.

Inside, it was cold. Older than cold. The kind of chill that comes not from air, but from time. The only furniture was a slab of iron in the center of the room, black with age. Around it, carved into the floor, a spiral of words:

*Speak, that the flame may sleep.*

The Reverend lit a lantern and hung it. Then he turned to me and said with a grim smile, "As fine a place for an end as one could wish."

I looked at him.

He smiled, faintly.

"You've felt it, haven't you? The weight. The watching. The Word scratching at the corners of your mind."

He stepped toward the slab. "Twenty-seven years ago, I came here. My preacher stood where I stand now. I watched him open the Book. I watched him speak until the blood ran from his nose. I watched the earth open and the fire speak back."

I swallowed.

"And I watched him step down into the hole."

I said nothing. My breath was shallow.

The Reverend placed his Bible on the slab.

"I preached that night. I preached until the crack closed. Until her voice fell silent again." He paused. "But not forever."

He stepped back and gestured for me to take his place.

# SPEAK, THAT THE FLAME MAY SLEEP

"Speak," he said. "Let the Word settle her."

I stepped forward, knees shaking. I opened my Bible… but the pages weren't right. The words shimmered and bent. Verses twisted into something darker.

Still, I began.

"My God is a fire…"

A groan beneath the floorboards. The spiral pulsed red, slow as breath.

"…and His flame burns the dross of the world…"

The slab of iron shifted. A line split down the middle.

I faltered. My voice broke.

The Reverend didn't move.

From the crack, a sound rose… wet, whispering, like a voice with too many mouths. The lantern flickered. The spiral glowed.

And then he stepped forward.

The Reverend.

He stepped onto the slab, into the widening crack.

He looked back at me. His eyes were black.

"*The flame chooses,*" he said, but it wasn't his voice.

Something inside him spoke now.

It smiled with his teeth.

I stumbled backward. The air swirled around him, thick and hot.

"*Speak,*" the voice said through him. "*Bind me again.*"

The Reverend reached for me.

His hand cracked at the wrist. His skin bubbled like old varnish.

And I knew.

*This was the inheritance.*

This was the end of his circuit, and the beginning of mine.

I raised my voice. Not scripture. Not verse.

Just words.

Fierce, raw, desperate.

"Be silent, beast! You are named! You are known! You are not welcome here!"

The slab shook.

The Reverend screamed... one long, spiraling howl.
I kept going.
"Return to the dust, to the deep, to the silence that bore you!"
His body bent backward, arms wide. His chest split with light.
It took a long time before he was fully consumed.

The world outside was still, the cold biting deeper than before, as if something beneath the soil had awakened and was watching. I dragged the Reverend's body to the edge of the clearing and buried him shallow, the earth reluctant to open, the roots twisted and black. I marked the grave with a stone, but even as I did, I felt the gesture was empty. The land here did not remember the dead kindly.

I saddled my horse and rode out alone, the circuit now mine.

Each town along the route seemed smaller, the faces in the pews more hollowed, their eyes fixed not on me, but on the chained Bible I carried. I preached, as the Reverend had, but the words no longer felt like mine. The scripture shifted beneath my tongue... verses bent, promises soured. I spoke of burdens and cleansing, of fire and silence, and watched as the congregation's fear deepened, their hope curdling into something like dread.

At night, I dreamed of the spiral carved in the chapel floor, of the iron slab and the crack that split the world. I dreamed of the Reverend's voice, now warped and echoing, urging me onward: "Speak, that the flame may sleep." But the flame did not sleep. It watched, hungry, patient.

I began to notice changes in myself. My prayers grew shorter, my silences longer. The Bible's pages grew slick and dark at the edges, the ink bleeding into strange, hungry shapes. Sometimes, when I spoke, I heard a second voice beneath my own—low, insistent, promising that the circuit would never end, only change hands.

## SPEAK, THAT THE FLAME MAY SLEEP

The people grew wary. Some stopped coming to the chapel. Others lingered after the service, eyes wide, lips moving in silent pleas. I could offer them nothing but the Word, and the Word was not what it had been.

One morning, as I prepared to ride the last leg of the circuit, I caught my reflection in a window. My eyes were rimmed with shadow, my mouth set in a line I recognized from the Reverend. I understood, then, that the spiral had already begun to turn within me.

The road led, inevitably, back to the lonely chapel at the world's end. I felt its pull—a promise, a curse. I knew, with a certainty that hollowed me out, that I would stand on that slab soon myself. That I would speak the words, and that the flame would choose.

And as I rode through the thinning mist, the Bible heavy in my saddlebag, I realized the truth the Reverend had carried in silence: the circuit does not save. It only feeds. And someday, when the spiral closed, I too would split with light, and another would inherit the burden.

*The Word is a sword. Speak with blood.*

The flame never truly sleeps.

# BUILD TO SUIT

## AMANDA DEBORD

"Dad? Dad!" Matty called out to me. "Can I pick out *any* room I want?"

"Yeah, Buddy. Any room. The whole house is ours."

"But not the master—" Amy started, then stopped, smiling at up at me. I knew that look. That *fuck-it* look. That *everything-is-going-so-good-so-who-cares?* look.

"Not the master, Matty," I shouted up the stairs. "The one with the attached bathroom is ours." I lean down and kiss Amy on the lips. An attached bathroom. A *second* bathroom. No more timing my shits so no one is waiting on me to get out.

"Well?" I asked. "Do you think we can make it out here? Think we can survive the commute?"

"Just let me enjoy my coffee on the deck and I can survive anything out here." Amy sighed. I knew she was already calculating how early she'd have to get up to get into her office on time. I was thankful for my telecommute.

"Dad I'm going outside to explore I'll be back later!" Matty shouted as he ran by.

Later that afternoon, Amy and I sat in the porch swing, dusty and tired from unpacking. Duck ran around his new yard, sniffing at every single thing. I could hear Matty's footsteps thundering through the house before he burst through the front door.

"Dad! I found another house!"

"Sorry, son." I clapped him on the shoulder. "All of our credit is tied up in this mortgage." The third glass of wine was starting to make me feel silly.

"No, like a rock house. Out in the woods. Like *old*. Indians or some shit."

"*Matt.*"

"Sorry, Dad." He looked at Amy. "But it's seriously old. You've got to come see it. There's a bunch of weird stuff drawn all over it."

Amy, of course, was up out of the swing before he even finished the sentence. I waved them off and leaned back, smiling to myself. Exploring the woods would be good for Matty. Get him off his phone for once. But I did wish the agent had told me there was a second structure on the property.

No use now. I poured another glass and patted myself on the back. I'd cut our mortgage by a third with this house. I could no longer hear the interstate from my bed. My new wife and my son were off on an adventure together. Life was alright for once.

# BUILD TO SUIT

"Lewis, you've really got to see it in real life," Amy said, scrolling through the pictures on the phone she'd set in front of me at the dinner table. "It was too dark to get good pictures of the inside, but it was incredible."

"It was like a hut, Dad. It just looked like an outhouse from the outside. But Amy shined her phone in it and there was no hole. It just went back and down and was just… empty. It was big inside."

"Big? Like how big?" I wondered if I could fit my mower in it. I squinted down at the tiny moss-covered stone shack on the screen. It looked barely big enough for two grown men to stand inside.

"Big," Amy echoed. "But kind of not. It's so narrow, and then you walk in and it slopes way down and just ends. It feels like it's supposed to go deeper, but it just ends. And get this. There's a window in the back wall, with nothing but dirt on the other side."

"It stunk, too," Matty added. "Like a basement."

I scrolled through her pictures. Zoomed in on one. The rocks were fitted expertly together, but looked uncut, like they'd been lifted whole out of the ground a hundred years ago. Rounded turd-shaped black smudges marred the outside. They looked like a child's drawings of too-fat snakes.

"Probably some kid's clubhouse. Or a deer blind. But I don't want you playing out there. Those rocks could fall anytime, and God only knows how much poison ivy is growing out there."

"But Dad! It's so cool! And it's right behind our house!"

"There's no poison ivy out there, Lewis," Amy said. "No bugs either. It would be a perfect place for a kid."

I pulled another slice of pizza onto my plate. The additional half-bottle of wine I'd had while they were out adventuring was making me feel annoyed with the whole thing. "I said no, Amy. I'd like my son to not die in a cave-in the first week I have him out of the city."

Then I felt bad. Not even twenty-four hours here and I was already strung out. But my tone didn't seem to bother the two of them. Amy took her phone back and she and Matty spent the rest of dinner zooming in on pictures, playing Indiana Jones and ignoring me.

"Alright. That'll be due back Wednesday by four p.m. Just bring it around back here and we'll check you in. Call us if you need an extra day, but don't bring it back late or we'll have to charge you double."

I watched as a man in coveralls with a nametag reading "Junior" drove the front-loader up on my trailer. *My* trailer, like I hadn't just bought it the day before. But here I was at Ozark Mountain Rentals pretending to be a mountain man. A mountain man who had *always* owned his own trailer and knew how to operate a front-loader but somehow didn't have a buddy who could lend him one.

As Junior lumbered back down the ramp, Buck handed me the clipboard for my signature. "What'cha diggin' out?"

"Oh, just some brush and an old stone pile out back of my property."

"That stone will bring a pretty penny with folks in town. Ladies like to use them in their flower gardens."

"Not these," I said as I handed him back the clipboard. "They're all misshapen and mossy. And they stink, too. Got an old hut or something out back of my house that somebody built before we bought the place. I'm afraid my kid's going to get hurt out there."

"Hut, you say?" Buck eyed my signature like he thought it might be fake. "Like from Indians? The university will want to know about that. You'll need a permit before you go messing around something like that out there."

"No. Not Indians. Just some kid making a playhouse or some old lady's fruit cellar. What's an Ind—*Native American*—want with a one-room hut that's half underground, anyway?" I put the pen to the paper to

BUILD TO SUIT

sign, but Buck jerked it out of my hand before I got through my first name.

"You can't just go around tearing down Indian structures out here." I watched as Junior sighed and trudged back up the trailer ramp and put the key back in the ignition.

"It's not Indian ... If you'd just—"

"I've got a buddy works over in the history department," Buck said as he pulled the phone from his pocket. "He'll know all about what you've got to do to get a permit to have that on your land."

"Permit to have it on my land?" I stepped toward him. "It was there before I bought the place! God knows how long it's been there!"

"Exactly!" Buck smiled. "Now hold on ..." He put up a finger to shush me, then spoke into the phone. "Yeah, Miles? It's Buck. I've got another of them huts for you to look at. Yeah, it's at"—he glanced down at my unsigned contract—"859 Clear Creek Road. Yeah. Uh-huh. I'll give him your number and—"

I got back in my car before he could finish and gave them both the finger out my window.

"You *what?*" Amy looked up from her computer. "They think it's an archaeological site and you didn't even look into it?"

"Amy, come on. You saw the place! It's as much an archaeological site as the Wal-Mart down the road. I'm sure ol' Buck in there gets a cut from whatever the county will want to charge me for a permit. It's all a big racket out here. They smell us outsiders coming as soon as we get off I-44 and then they just line up for their piece of the pie."

I was still fuming as I remembered sitting awkwardly in my car while I waited for Junior to drive the machine back down off my trailer.

"Shouldn't you at least *check* to see it's not something historical?"

"Amy. Are you honestly that naïve? I know you're excited about the romance of living in the woods but come on. This is our property now. *Ours.* Just like you said *you* wanted. I'm not leaving some crooked pile of rocks out there for Matty to get buried in, even if Pocahontas herself built it."

Amy just looked at me. Silent. Like she does.

"What? Why are you looking at me like that?"

"Pocahontas? Really? We've been out here less than a week, Lewis, and you're already starting to sound like one of the locals."

"What's that supposed to mean?"

"A little racist, don't you think? Before long, you'll be flying the stars and bars."

*Racist. Intolerant. Ignorant.* That self-hating talk was just one more reason I was happy to get out of the city. I'm not racist, not by a long way, but I did relish the idea of sitting on the porch with a beer and not wondering who my neighbors voted for or if I'd done enough to atone for my great grandparents' sins.

I stormed out back of the house, toward the rock hut. I'd hoped to spend my day razing it and then using the stones to line our driveway. But now here I was on foot, no loader, and with no plan for the afternoon other than going over the scenes with Buck and with Amy in my mind.

*Stupid fucking pile of rocks.* I kicked at it. *Some hillbilly builds a doghouse out of scraps he probably stole from the quarry and suddenly we've got to call the Smithsonian before we piss within a one-mile radius.*

I kicked at it again and one of the stones tumbled loose. Some Indian architecture. I doubted this thing could have stood for twelve solid months, let alone centuries.

But I had to admit, it did look taller than when I'd come out here the first time. The angles at the corners were neat and square, like someone had come by and straightened them. It was something I could imagine Matty and Amy doing together, an hour or so of tedium just to aggravate me.

*Doesn't matter*, I thought as I kicked at it again and two more good-sized stones fell. *It's coming down.*

That night, Amy and I sat by the fire, our first night alone in the house. Matty was at his mom's, and I'd hoped there'd be some romance. But Amy was absorbed in her book, *Native Rock Structures of the Ozarks*. I was proud of my hard work kicking it over and sorting the rocks into piles by size, but I didn't tell her what I'd done. The gin and tonic in my hand tasted like triumph, though.

Monday morning, Amy buzzed around the kitchen getting ready for work. She grabbed the handful of mail out of the box by the door and tossed it on the table in front of me. Bills. Bills. Refinance offers. An envelope from the University of the Ozarks. I tore it open as Amy paused at the storm door.

Dear Mr. Keltner,

> My apologies for the intrusion. I was given your name and address by Bernard ("Buck," as you likely know him) Parson. He informed me that you have found a primitive hut on your land that may be Indigenous in origin. Such structures are of great archaeological and cultural importance, and I would love the opportunity to come out and investigate your findings in person. Unfortunately, I am on sabbatical this semester and will be out of the country for the next several weeks.

If you're willing, it would benefit my research greatly if you would take pictures of the structure, from as many angles as possible, and send them, along with a rough sketch of the hut and the surrounding geography, indicating approximate dimension, to my email address listed below. Please pay special attention to any markings on the outside of the structure.

Based on Bernard's description, I believe the hut to be of Osage origin, though it may be even older.

Best regards,
    Miles Hubbard, Ph.D.
    Professor of Ancient Archaeology
    University of the Ozarks

"Older than the Osage?" Amy gasped, reading over my shoulder. "But they were here in like the 1600s. He thinks it might be older than that? Jesus, Lewis. What are we living on?"

"Amy. You can't be serious. You think this is for real? You think we happened to luck into an archaeological find *ten miles from town*, in a house built in the 1950s? No one has ever mentioned it before, but suddenly the new kid from St. Louis discovers it and now they think it's a major historical discovery? Or do you think they see a chance to fleece the city boy and make a few bucks while reminding us that we're not from here?"

"Lewis, I swear. You sound just like those conspiracy nuts you're always making fun of. Not everyone is out to get you. How hard can it be to send the guy a few pictures? It's not harming anything. And if they think it really is something, you can fence it off and make them take care of the mowing around it!"

She was giving me that look again. That *I know you think this is bullshit, but I think you should do it anyway* look. And I knew from experience that look wasn't followed far behind by the *I'll do it my damn self* look, and I couldn't have her going out there and seeing what I'd done to it. So I grabbed my phone and a notebook and laced up my boots.

"Have a nice day at work, honey!" Amy said as she breezed back out the door.

When I stood in front of the hut, I realized I hadn't yet decided what I thought I was going to take pictures of, or what I was going to tell Amy when she got home, but I'd known for sure I wasn't going to be sending squat to Miles Hubbard, Ph.D.

But here it stood in front of me. Four straight stone walls. Rebuilt. As sturdy as can be. The stones were even put back so that the drawings lined up just like they had before.

I circled it, fuming. *Fuckers.* Someone was having me on. They'd seen me kick it down and they put it back together just so I'd have to own up to it. But two could play at that game. I leaned in hard to it with my shoulder, grunting and pushing against the mossy rocks until they groaned and started to give way again. The cold musty smell drifted up through the widening cracks between the stones.

I pulled my shirt up over my nose. Something smelled rotten inside. The thought of an animal getting trapped down inside there only strengthened my resolve to have this thing gone. What if Duck got stuck down there? Or Matty, God forbid? Heaven only knew what sort of rot there was in there. What sort of tetanus crept up the dank walls.

But then it came to me. *Matty.* The poor kid was dying for his own space. Even in our bigger house, he was pulling away, pushing us back. What thirteen-year-old wants to hang around his dad and stepmom in the first place? He probably thought this could be his teenage man-cave, a place to hide a joint and a stack of *Hustlers*, maybe.

# AMANDA DEBORD

    I felt for him, I did.

    I kicked and pushed at the walls with renewed strength until they crumbled and I resolved to level this place out, build a lean-to with Matty in the springtime, or maybe even buy a little camper. Every boy needs a hideaway to call his own.

*\<Hey Matty\>*

*\<...\>*

*\<Hey I'm sorry, but I had to take down the stone hut again. I know it probably took you all weekend to stack those rocks back up. But it's just not safe out there.\>*

*\<I'm afraid you'll get buried.\>*

*\<But you did an amazing job with it.\>*

*\<Matty.\>*

*\<You there?\>*

*\<...\>*

                                        *\<What are you talking about? What do you mean again?\>*

*\<The hut. It's ok. I know you put it back up.\>*

                                                                    *\<I didn't touch it\>*

*\<I'm not mad.\>*

                                *\<I didn't touch it. It was up when I was there last weekend\>*

*\<...\>*

                                                                       *\<Dad?\>*

# BUILD TO SUIT

I bought a cheap trail cam at Wally-world the next day. My fingers itched. I couldn't wait to catch whoever it was. I considered hiding out there, catching it all on camera when I scared the shit out of them. Maybe put it on YouTube.

But then maybe I'd catch something else. What if it wasn't just one person? What if it was a group? A *coven*? I pictured people dressed in black, carrying black candles and making those weird symbols. So close to our house. What if they were watching us?

But I never caught anything. Morning after morning I checked the feed and... nothing. Nothing but a black-and-white still-life of tumbled-down rocks and bare branches that blew in the wind. Sometimes if I watched it long enough, I felt like I could see white shapes moving around the shadows, but it was just the pixels in the grainy video.

Eventually I stopped checking every day.

Weeks went past.

Life moved on.

One snowy afternoon in early December, there was a knock. Duck jumped in surprise, then ran to the door, his nails clicking on the linoleum as he tried to nose open the door. I closed my laptop and went to the kitchen door and was greeted by none other than Miles Hubbard, Ph.D., himself. He must have read the annoyance on my face because he smiled extra big. I could see his teeth.

"Mr. Keltner!" he said through the storm door before I even opened it. "I'm sorry to bother you at home. I've sent you a number of letters. Left voicemail."

I left the storm door shut. I wanted to see how long until he got the hint.

"I heard back from my colleagues in Virginia. They were stunned by the pictures I sent them. Stunned, Mr. Keltner. You see, the pictographs. Well, they're common for the Osage of the Ozark region, well-known, even, but …" He paused. "I'm sorry, Mr. Keltner, but may I come in? This really is a matter of great importance to the scientific community."

I swear I felt my eye twitch when he said that, but there was something about his sincerity. He was so excited, he was flushed. Or was that something other than excitement? I saw the dampness at the armpits of his button-up, even in this cold.

"Yes, please come in," I offered. "Lewis."

"Pardon?"

"Lewis. My name. You can call me Lewis."

I got Miles a cup of coffee and sat him down at my kitchen table and he talked. I had to admire his enthusiasm, really. I don't know when was the last time I got that excited about my job. Miles brought books with him. And file folders. And he showed me picture after picture of stone hut after stone hut. They all looked like the one in my yard, which confused me even more.

"If there are so many of these, why are you all worked up about this one? It sounds like they're all over the place out here."

"Well they are, Mr—Lewis," Miles stuttered. "But yours is different. See? Look at the interior pictures of these. You can even see it a little from the outside." He spread three photographs out in front of me.

"I'm sorry. I don't see it."

"Look at the angles, Lewis. They're all sloping upward. They all face east and slope upward, toward the sun. Some of them even have small holes built into the back wall so that the sun shines directly in on the spring equinox. We believe part of the function of the huts was to act as a sort of ritual calendar." He sipped his coffee.

"But *your* hut. Your wife said it herself. It slopes down, into the earth. By the time you reach the back wall, you're almost entirely underground. Her pictures don't show, of course, whether there's a viewing window on that wall, but I have my suspicions. It's a direct perversion of every other hut I've seen, and I want to know why."

"You got a coat?" I asked, standing up.

"Pardon me?"

"A coat? You got one? If you're going to interrupt my afternoon, you may as well go out and look at it. But I'm afraid you're going to be disappointed."

"Disappointed? How?"

"Well, something's taken it down. It's been knocked down since August."

"Lewis. I'm afraid I don't understand what you're saying."

"Down. Wrecked. Maybe some kids or something, but it's been leveled. I didn't get any of your letters or phone calls, but I would have loved to have told you before you wasted your gas on a trip out here. The hut is gone, Miles."

"But that's not possible."

"I'm sorry to say it, but it's true. I guess you can load up the rocks for your lab if you—"

"No, I mean, nothing tore it down, Mr. Keltner. I was just out there. Forgive me," he muttered. "I shouldn't have been on your property without your permission, but I was just so eager to see it, I… well I went out there first. And as of about fifteen minutes ago, it was still standing. But what I wanted to ask you, Mr. Keltner, was about the door."

"The door?"

"The wooden door at the entrance to the structure. Did you build that? It's certainly stunning craftsmanship, but it's clearly modern. I have to advise you that defacing or altering a recognized Indigenous structure in such a way, even on your own property, can carry a heavy penalty. Now I don't think—"

I didn't hear what he said after that, but I could hear his voice behind me as I paced through the backyard and he struggled to keep up. Sure enough, there it stood. Rebuilt. With a wooden door and iron hinges and another of those infernal worms carved into the timber of the door.

I'm sure my name is in a university report somewhere for the impoliteness I showed when shooing Miles Hubbard off my property, but I couldn't care less.

As soon as I heard his tires moving down the gravel driveway, I opened my laptop back up. I brought up the trail cam feed and my stomach flipped over. The video still showed a pile of stones, just like I'd left them. It must have stopped recording sometime and I never noticed. How long? For how long had I been looking at a still photograph of a pile of rocks? How many nights had Amy and Matty and I slept peacefully in our beds with who knows who out there, building. And for what? Why us? Why this land?

I'd had enough. I looked at the clock on the kitchen stove. 2:30. Amy would be home in two hours. Matty would be here at 6:00. I whistled for Duck. We were not going to sleep another night with fucking *Satanists* partying in the backyard.

I changed my boots, put my coat back on, and headed out to the garage for the gas can. As I walked out the kitchen door, I spared one more glance at my laptop screen, at the pile of tumbled-down rocks and the leaf-bare tree branches swaying in the wind, the snow swirling around. What was I missing?

I was in there for a very long time, I think. I never intended to go inside. But I had to look, had to open the door. I wanted to see the back wall, buried underground, with my own eyes.

I just couldn't figure why they'd build a door when the space inside was as small as it was, and all it did was lead to a dead end in the dirt. Why bother trying to keep anything out, or in? I set my gas can down outside and pushed the door. The hinges creaked and I stepped inside the cold, dark room. Something dripped under the floor. And there was that clicking noise again. Duck snuffed at the floor and whined.

It took a few moments for my eyes to adjust to the dark. I wish they never had. I wish I'd never seen that hut, never seen the hole in the back wall and the window that looked out into nothing. I wish I could have clawed my eyes out instead of seeing what was squeezing itself through that window. I don't want to remember the size of the room, impossible, or the sound I heard when that *thing* plopped on the floor.

I can still see it now, even if I close my eyes. It was as if I could feel it, lurching and clicking, thick and white along the stone floor. A fat white grub that wheezed and pulsed. And with every whistling breath it grew fatter, thicker.

I can hear it breathing as I run back through the dark woods. How is it dark already? I made it back to the house, somehow, but it's very, very dark. I can barely see. The light switch doesn't work. If it's this dark, it's late, and Matty should be here. Amy should have been home a long time ago. Maybe she is here. Someone is in here with me. I call out for her, but I can't hear my own voice. I start to think I've been calling for her for a long time.

I've had a lot of time to think about it, about what I saw inside, and about what I caught, or didn't catch, on my trail cam. If I'd paused for a moment when I left my kitchen earlier today (or whenever it was, I can't remember anymore), I would have seen the pile of stones like I'd left them, and I would have seen the trees swaying and the snow whispering around the rocks. I figured the camera hadn't been working, had frozen on a still shot. If I'd watched and seen the trees swaying and the snow whispering around the rocks, I would have seen that it was recording just fine.

I should check again, but my laptop isn't sitting on the counter anymore. Nothing in this house is where I left it. I'm not sure I'd want to see what's on the screen anyway.

Matty sits in his room, hunched over his tablet. Mom let him stay home from school again today. He can see Dad again today, on the video. Mom refuses to look anymore. She turns her head when Matty talks about it. She never sees it. Sometimes it's too grainy. Once it was snowing too hard. Some days, and those are the days when Matty feels like he's going to go crazy himself, the feed only shows a pile of rocks, becoming increasingly covered with moss and dead dry leaves.

But today the hut is standing and today he can see Dad. He knows it's him by the way he's standing inside the doorway. Dad hasn't moved for a very long time now, and Matty wants to scream at him through the screen. He knows what happens next, after Dad has stood there for so long.

Soon his father's mouth will open wide, his eyes wide, and his hands will claw at the side of his face. If Matty can keep from turning away (sometimes he can't), he'll watch as worm after thick, white worm spills from Lewis's mouth and wriggles off into the woods.

# UNDERFOOT OF THE GOWROW

## D.R. COOK (AND HIS CAT)

**Underfoot of Greatness**
*Little Rock, Arkansas*
*October 23rd, 1897, 10:17 AM*

Urya Underfoot's whiskers twitched, alive with the palpable excitement in the air. The scent of rodent fear and fresh blood permeated the roof of her mouth, a delicious promise. It couldn't hide from her, despite its desperate efforts.

Every time it scrabbled deeper into the shed's wooden wall, it made just enough sound for Urya to almost see it in her mind's eye, a tiny, vibrating tremor in the unseen darkness. *Right there*, she thought, muscles coiling, as she prepared to launch her ambush.

A flicker of movement. A tiny, panicked squeak. Urya launched herself, a blur of feline grace, spreading daggered claws. The kill was swift—a loud, desperate squeak, then silence—and deeply satisfying to Urya's inner huntress. The warmth of the small body pulsed in her jaws. One. A good start. Her humans would be pleased. Urya clutched her prize, already moving to show off her contribution to the family.

With her prize held limply in her maw, Urya made her way to the cart. Slipping from the familiar smells of horse dung and hay in the barn, she deftly navigated toward her Master's horse-drawn wagon.

William Miller, the Master, was already loading chest after heavy chest into it, his large frame blocking the light. He was speaking to another human, a safe human whose scent was familiar, one who visited sometimes, a *neighbor*, she thought the Master called him once.

Urya listened carefully as the humans made their strange, vibrating sounds to each other. Though she couldn't understand the exact meaning of their guttural purrs and spits, she pretended to, just in case one looked down, so she could present what truly mattered: food.

"So you are really going there to investigate this strange beast, William?" the neighbor's voice rumbled, laced with a mix of disbelief and eager curiosity.

"Well," William Miller rumbled back, his gaze drifting into the hazy distance, as if seeing beyond the immediate woods. "I am going up that way anyway. We're thinking of expanding the logging crew in that direction. There's some truly magnificent timber in that area, a vast, untouched stand of white oaks with trunks wide enough to build a small house, and towering shortleaf pines that reach for the sky. Perfect for sturdy lumber, railroad ties, and the kind of dense, hard wood that holds up for generations."

He paused, a scent of satisfaction emanating from him. "That kind of asset is hard to come by these days, especially with so much land already claimed."

# UNDERFOOT OF THE GOWROW

The neighbor, however, didn't vibrate with interest about Miller Lumber & Timber Co.'s latest asset deep in Blanco County. His attention was fixed on the monstrous, lizard-like beast that had been spotted in that tiny town.

"Did you take your Kodak just in case you do see it? Perhaps if you can be brave enough, you might even get a photograph." The last word came out roughly, as if the man rarely used such a modern term.

William did not reply with more of his strange human sounds. Instead, he simply lifted a wooden box from a crate, revealing a dark, glass eye. He showed it to the neighbor, then returned it to its protective casing.

Urya could no longer wait for her Master to stop vibrating the air with his purrs and spits. She decided to pull off her signature move. Any time she wanted attention, she knew exactly how to "accidentally" trip a human by sweeping through their legs. They would immediately take notice and call her last name.

With a silent, sleek dart, Urya wove between William Miller's legs just as he turned from the cart. His boot caught her, not hard enough to truly hurt, but enough to send him stumbling, a loud grunt escaping his chest. He flailed, catching himself on the side of the wagon, his face contorted in a mix of surprise and annoyance.

"Urya! You little menace!" William Miller's booming voice, usually a comfort, was sharp with irritation. "Always underfoot, aren't you? That's it, you're Urya Underfoot, always living up to your name!"

He glared down, and that's when his gaze landed on the small, limp mouse, still clutched proudly in Urya's jaw. His face, already red from the near fall, twisted into a grimace of pure disgust. "Ugh! Get that filthy thing out of here!" He made a shooing motion with his foot, sending a wave of unpleasant vibrations through the ground.

Urya flattened herself, a low growl rumbling in her chest, not from fear of the Master's voice, but from the lingering scent of danger that still pricked at her nose. The humans were loud, clumsy, and often oblivious. They didn't understand the true threats that stalked the edges of their world.

But the Master, despite his momentary anger, was the strongest human. He commanded others. He would go where the danger was, and she, Urya Underfoot, would go with him. She would endure the discomfort of the journey, the jostling, the strange smells of the road, because the alternative, the vast, ancient, wrong smell that still haunted the edges of her senses, was far, far worse. The terrible beast that made the *gowrow* sound late at night.

## Under the Foot of the Ozark
*Calf Creek Township, Blanco County, Arkansas*
*Deep within a hidden Ozark cave*
*October 23rd, 1897, 5:15 PM*

The Gowrow moved her immense, scaly body across the rough cave floor, a low rumble vibrating deep in her chest. The vibration intensified, blossoming into sound as she uttered her name: "GOOOOOW... RRROOOOW!"

Her ancient voice box cracked the silent air of the cave, the sound echoing off the walls, making the entire cavern seem to crescendo with her terrifying roar. Dust motes danced in the faint light filtering from the entrance, stirred by the sheer force of her bellow. Her destination: the entrance, where the ancient, fallen pine carcasses guarded the opening, hiding her lair from the outside world.

With her belly distended from a recent kill, and her webbed, clawed hands effortlessly pushing aside the gnawed bones of previous dinners, the creature reached the mouth of the cave. She lifted her massive head, her nostrils flaring, eager to taste the currents of the outside air.

She froze, every primal instinct deciphering the airborne messages. The scent of white-tailed deer, her usual food source, was still running low, but there was an even stronger smell of the humans who also fed on them.

Humans made terrible prey themselves and competed for the deer. The Gowrow killed any human she could find alone, consuming them as was her right, even if she didn't truly enjoy the flavor.

The wind also carried the large horse smell—delicious, but they ran quickly and, if provoked, could put up a fight, so not worth the effort. Now, the smaller, horse-like creatures the humans called "dogs" were another matter. More like crunchy, yummy wolves, with a playful, easily dismissed bite. Their tiny nips barely even hurt; she wasn't sure how such creatures dared to try in the rough neighborhood of the Ozarks. She didn't know, and she didn't care. She was just glad they were there for a snack when she needed them.

Now, the smaller, quicker "dogs" the humans called "cats"—they were another story. Like bobcats or mountain lions, they hunted just like her, but they were far more stealthy. Sure, they were yummy like the dogs, but their tiny claws did cause her pain.

The memory of the most recent encounter flared, a painful lesson she would not forget, for pain was to be avoided. But not lunch. So she decided on a dog for the evening, or perhaps, if she worked herself up to it, a cow. Oh, the cows. Cows were the things she daydreamed of.

She entertained such thoughts as she sharpened her bottom tusks against the rough granite walls of her lair, the stone groaning faintly under the pressure. In her mind's eye, she could smell a cat, but not just any cat—a cat that was traveling on a wagon. A scent she would smell again in days to come, a meal that, given the choice, she would savor as her condemned murder victim's last. She sounded her name and let out a fearsome "GGGOOOWWWRRROOOOWWW!!!!!!"

D.R. COOK

**Under the Foot of the Pub**
*Calf Creek Township, Arkansas*
*October 23rd, 1897, 6:30 PM*

How in the name of the Egyptian goddess Bast did humans ever hunt any prey, or even survive this feline-ruled world, when their sounds disturbed even the chosen species'—cats'—dreams? Urya had cocooned herself into the contents of the Master's horse-drawn cart, a perfect, fluid, grey-furry egg yolk, with the bags and travel chests acting as sound barriers to the new, overwhelming noises.

As the cart rumbled into the township, a cacophony assaulted her sensitive ears: the sharp clatter of a blacksmith's hammer, the distant *thump-thump* of a lumber mill, and the high-pitched, insistent *caw-caw-caw* of agitated chickens. The air thickened with a jumble of new scents: stale woodsmoke, the acrid tang of human sweat, the sweet-sour smell of fermenting fruit from a hidden still, and the rich, earthy aroma of freshly turned soil.

In her purrfect dream, she was ruler of a mouse-based kingdom, long established but forgotten to the real world of feline dominance. There, she and she alone was queen, swiftly devouring her rebellious subjects and generously rewarding the survivors with their lives if they brought her cream and their young. To be a goddess!

But then, a sudden, piercing *WHOOOOOSH-CLANG!*—the shriek of a steam whistle, followed by the deafening thrum of heavy machinery—tore through her royal, fragile egg dream, thrusting her into the noisy reality of humans and their strange, jarring sounds.

Urya made the choice to get her land legs back after traveling so far on the Master's weird transport. She hit the ground quietly, a silent landing, but she almost slipped—a miscalculation in her feline brain.

The ground here was different: packed dirt, rough cobbles, not the soft earth she was used to. So too were the sounds, of course, and the smells. The scent that intrigued her most, however, was the lingering

# UNDERFOOT OF THE GOWROW

musk of a predatory reptile, one that had obviously been haunting moldy, damp caves.

She had smelled it faintly at home, a scent that had triggered something deep inside her. It was the feeling of when her mother had carried her by the scruff when she was young, the thrill of her first kill, the chilling memory of seeing one of her kind stop moving and become dinner themselves to insects or other predators. Something she could not name, a primal instinct, as humans would say, but they were too often blinded by their own flawed thinking to truly understand.

Yes, that smell was here, strong and deep, weaving through the woods and circling the township. Her instinct was to run into the Ozark forest, to find the creature, to warn her Master, and even stop it if she could. But hunger had other plans, reminding her of the rich smells from the pub—the promise of free floor beer and all the fat rats a cat could catch.

She changed her mind, and, with a silent, graceful movement, she slipped through the swinging doors of the tavern behind her Master, who was making that weird sound again. The one that put her hackles on edge. *Gowrow*.

"Good to see you again, Mr. Miller! How goes the lumber business?" the large, food-smelling man, whose name Urya now associated with "Matthew," boomed at her Master.

"Wonderful, Matthew!" William Miller replied, his own voice booming, a sound that made the air vibrate with satisfaction. He removed his hat and coat, handing them to Matthew to hang up. "Since the last time we talked, I did indeed buy some of this land, just as we discussed. I'm proud to announce you can now inform your pub customers that there are lumberjack jobs available, at double the pay! Two dollars and fifty cents a day!"

"Then your drinks and supper are on me!" Matthew boomed back, his laugh a deep, rumbling sound. He had more facial hair than grace, and his scent was a mix of stale beer and fresh cooking.

Urya ignored all the weird humans now, their loud sounds and confusing scents, in favor of her favorite meal. The rats and mice here were indeed well-fed and plump; she could tell by their droppings, which carried the rich scent of discarded human food. She sought them out beneath the floorboards, an area she could just barely reach by becoming her liquid form, flowing through the smallest gaps.

While she hunted, her laser-like feline focus didn't let her daydream. But after a few meals were consumed, and she was meticulously cleaning the fresh, delicious blood off her paws, she was able to ruminate on the reptilian smell. Why did it bother her so? She heard her Master in the distance making that weird sound again, the one that perked up her ears. She used her goddess-given feline focus to try to decode what the humans were saying to each other now.

"So, Miller, you truly aimin' to cut timber out in the Blanco hollers?" a gruff voice rumbled, smelling of stale pipe smoke and skepticism. "Heard tell that land's been trouble. Livestock gone missing, and not just from wolves."

"Aye," another voice, sharper, chimed in. "Old Man Higgins lost a whole cow last week. Found naught but a mess of torn-up earth and a peculiar smell. Said it weren't no bear."

William Miller's voice, usually so confident, vibrated with a new, almost eager tension. "Just rumors, gentlemen. Wild tales. The land's rich with timber, and that's what I'm after. A beast, you say? Well, a beast is just a bigger varmint, easily dealt with."

He let out a dismissive huff, but Urya, from her vantage point beneath the floor, could detect a subtle shift in his scent—a new, sharp tang of curiosity, almost a challenge.

"They say it's got tusks," a younger voice, smelling of nervous sweat, whispered. "And a tail like a blade. Comes from the caves, they say. Makes a sound that'll curdle your blood."

Then, the swinging door of the tavern creaked open, admitting a gust of cold air and the fresh, earthy scent of the woods. A small boy, no older than the master's son, Thomas, stumbled in, his eyes wide, clutching two freshly killed rabbits. His scent was a mix of youthful fear

# UNDERFOOT OF THE GOWROW

and the sharp, metallic tang of fresh blood.

"Mr. Miller! Mr. Miller!" the boy gasped, his voice thin and reedy, vibrating with a frantic energy. "I was out by the old creek bed, near the big rock overhang, and I saw 'em! Tracks! Bigger than any bear, with three toes, like a lizard! And a long scrape beside 'em, like somethin' dragged a giant knife!"

Urya froze. Tracks. Three toes. Lizard. Scrape. Her ears swiveled, processing the boy's frantic purrs. She understood. She had been spending too much time with the humans.

**Under the Foot of Prey**
*Ozark Wilderness, Blanco County, Arkansas*
*October 23rd, 1897, 7:05 PM*

The Gowrow did not appreciate the juvenile human trying to track her. She had considered hunting it down and consuming it along with the rabbit snacks it carried, but the Gowrow was still full from the calf she had blood-drunkly consumed. Her tusks were still slick with the remnants of her kill, a beautiful, glistening reminder of her power.

The calf had been a simple, satisfying hunt. Its panicked bleats had been a brief, sharp song in the twilight, quickly muffled as the Gowrow's massive jaws clamped down. The warmth of its blood had flooded her throat, thick and rich, filling her belly with a heavy, contented weight. The snapping of bone, the tearing of muscle—a symphony of consumption.

She had dragged the carcass deep into a shadowed hollow, tearing away the choicest cuts before settling down to gnaw lazily on a femur, savoring the marrow.

Now, while munching idly on some remaining cow bones, the Gowrow caught the distinct scent of the human child. It wasn't running away, nor was it moving toward any of the Gowrow's usual snares. This scent was moving toward her. A flicker of annoyance, then a predatory calculation. The Gowrow decided to meet her pursuer head-on, not for a meal, but to scare it away, to make it drop its paltry offerings.

She moved with a low, silent slither, her heavy scales scraping faintly against the damp earth. On the top of the Ozark mountain hill, silhouetted against the fading light, the Gowrow saw the boy. The child was looking straight down at his feet, or rather, at the ground directly in front of his feet. He was meticulously studying the Gowrow's tracks, as if he were the hunter.

If it had not been for the cold fall air, and the cold blood that flowed through the Gowrow's ancient veins, she would have been warm with pure, indignant rage. How dare this small, soft creature presume to track her?

The child, suddenly sensing her immense presence, darted away, sprinting off in the direction of the other humans, his scent now laced with raw terror. The Gowrow let him go. She could pick up another smell now, a small, ugly "dog" the humans called a "cat."

Not just any cat, but a specific cat. She had smelled it a long time ago, in a dream perhaps, or just yesterday—the Gowrow didn't know and didn't care. It was a unique, intriguing scent, and it was moving. She began to make her way toward the smell, her low, guttural roar echoing her name into the night sky.

**Under the Foot of the Ozark**
*Calf Creek Township, Blanco County, Arkansas*
*October 23rd, 1897, 7:05 PM*

Urya's day had been filled with sun-dappled, lazy cart rides, a cacophony of new smells, a constant blur of human movement, and an undercurrent of their strange excitement. She understood the men were taking their hard sticks—their long, loud-smelling weapons—and were heading out to hunt the creature their youngling had warned them of.

The youngling did indeed look like a smaller version of Master Thomas. He didn't smell quite the same but still had the same clumsy strokes on her fur that had messed up her meticulous grooming job.

She listened carefully as the humans made a game plan, their body language and exaggerated movements giving away their intentions, despite her not speaking human.

The farmer's frantic, booming voice overtook all other sounds in the pub. "This thing has ate enough of my cattle! Tonight, it meets our Lord and Savior Jesus!" His scent was thick with fear and righteous anger.

Other voices joined, a chorus of sharp, grief-filled purrs and bitter spits. A man smelling of old leather and desperation spoke of his prize hunting dog, its scent now gone from the woods, replaced only by a peculiar, foul musk. A woman, her voice a low, broken hum, spoke of her milk cow, found mangled and half-eaten, its familiar warmth turned to cold, bloody decay.

Then, a quiet, almost imperceptible lament from a corner, a scent of profound sorrow: a small baby, stillborn shortly after the creature's attacks began, as if the very air had been poisoned by its presence.

Urya watched all this with great boredom. She already knew what she must do. The old, moldy cave-reptile smell was coming closer, growing stronger with each gust of wind that snaked through the cracks in the pub walls.

She waited for an outside door to open, a brief gap in the human barrier. When it did, she slipped out like a thief in the night, a grey shadow melting into the deeper gloom. Above her, the Arkansas moon, a thin, silver sliver in the vast, inky sky, offered little light, but enough for a hunter like Urya.

The cold air tried its best to find its way past her majestic fur coat, but it failed in its attempt this time. Urya, truly earning her name now, sprinted through the old township, past horse tracks and dung, past human food smells and wooden signs hung. She darted past rancid, small outhouses where flies congregated and into the forested sections of the Ozark mountains.

She was a messenger, a message that must be sent to this new, crazed, musky cryptid. The message: *leave my humans alone*. This fluid, frantic scramble from small township to rocky, mountainous forest, made Urya seem like a silver-grey bullet in hunt of a lycanthrope who hid among the dark, gnarled trees.

Urya was close to her new adversary; she could smell her. She climbed a tree, her claws finding purchase on the rough bark, and dared to peek in that direction.

Below her, a monstrous form moved. Its body was immense, a long, low bulk of mottled greens and browns, like shadows come alive, covered in scales that glinted faintly even in the near darkness.

It moved with a heavy, scraping sound, a low *shhh-thump* as its powerful, short legs carried its weight. Its head, disproportionately large, swayed with a slow, deliberate rhythm, its nostrils flaring, tasting the air. From its upper jaw, two enormous, curving tusks, pale against its dark hide, jutted forward, sharp and ancient. Its tongue, a thick, dark ribbon, flicked out, tasting the air, then retracted with a wet *schlick*.

Along its spine, she could make out jagged, horn-like spikes, like broken tree branches, adding to its terrifying silhouette. Its tail, long and whip-like, dragged behind it, leaving a faint, disturbing scrape on the ground, the blade at its tip glinting with a cold, dull light. Its eyes, deep-set and dark, seemed to absorb the scant moonlight, reflecting nothing back. It was a creature of primal force, a living, breathing shadow.

Urya knew what it was thinking: *Prey. Easy. Mine*. The Gowrow was assessing, calculating, sensing the smaller creatures around it. It was a hunter, just like Urya, but on a scale that made her feel impossibly small, impossibly fragile. Urya Underfoot knew it would take a lot of courage to get underfoot of this devil.

# UNDERFOOT OF THE GOWROW

**Under Foot of the Pale Moonlight**
*Ozark Wilderness, Blanco County, Arkansas*
*October 23rd, 1897, 7:25 PM*

The Gowrow smelled a faint, intriguing scent, but now it was closer, bolder. A game of olfactory chess, a complex dance of airborne messages that humans, with their blunt, useless noses, would never be able to wrap their tiny monkey minds around. Since Mother Nature was cruel enough to leave them without working smelling receptors, they stumbled through the world, oblivious.

The Gowrow knew the cat was heading straight for her, and with intent. The cat, like the human child before, seemed so brazen, so utterly disrespectful.

The Gowrow rumbled low in her chest, a sound of ancient indignation. Her existence in these Ozark hills stretched back further than the oldest pine, longer than the oldest human memory. She remembered when the land was truly hers, when the only two-legged creatures were the dark-skinned natives. They moved with a quiet reverence, understanding the whispers of the forest, taking only what they needed. They respected the old ways, the old powers.

But these paler humans, they made more noise, trampled without thought, and had even less respect for her. They were invaders, carving out chunks of her domain for their noisy mills and stinking towns.

She was the undisputed apex predator of these hollows, a queen of tooth and claw, scale and tusk. Other creatures knew their place. The deer, swift and skittish, provided sustenance. The bears, clumsy and strong, usually kept to their own territories.

She remembered one such bear, a massive black brute, years ago. She had encountered it by a berry patch, both drawn by the sweet, ripe fruit. It had roared, a challenge, its fur bristling. She had lunged, tusks aimed, but the bear was a whirlwind of brute force, its thick hide deflecting her blows, its paws delivering crushing, unexpected impacts. The pain had been a shock, a searing humiliation. She had retreated, a rare, bitter taste of defeat. It was a lesson learned: even the strongest had to choose their battles. But this cat… this tiny, arrogant cat…

Urya, a silver-grey blur, dropped from the pine bough, a silent missile of fur and fury. Her claws, sharp as tiny daggers, raked across the Gowrow's massive, scaly back, finding purchase on the jagged, horn-like spikes along her spine. It wasn't a deep wound, not to the Gowrow, but it was a shock, an insult.

The Gowrow recoiled, a sudden, sharp pain lancing through her. She roared, a sound of pure, unadulterated agony and outrage: "GOOOOOW…RRROOOOWWW!!!"

This time, the cry was laced with a raw, unexpected vulnerability, echoing across the hills, alerting the approaching mob of townsfolk, led by William Miller, to the area. The Gowrow smelled them now, a wave of human scents—fear, anger, the metallic tang of their crude weapons. The air vibrated with their heavy footsteps, their frantic purrs.

This was no longer a simple hunt. This was an invasion. The Gowrow knew the safest place. Her webbed claws, designed for swift, silent passage through water, were her escape. With a quiet, powerful surge, she made a soft plop into the dark, cold waters of the Buffalo River, disappearing beneath the surface without a trace.

Urya landed lightly on the damp earth, her fur bristling, her breath coming in short, sharp gasps. She watched the disturbed water, then turned, her ears swiveling. She could hear the humans now, closer, their loud, clumsy sounds growing. She sat patiently, meticulously cleaning the invisible dust from her paws, waiting for her Master to return.

# UNDERFOOT OF THE GOWROW

**Under Foot and Over Hand**
*Calf Creek Township, Blanco County, Arkansas*
*October 23rd, 1897, 9:24 PM*

Urya followed her Master, who had collected a pride of his own. These humans, so loud, so clumsy, yet in their numbers they carried a strange, formidable scent of collective purpose. Their heavy boots crunched on the damp earth, a rhythmic *thump-thump-thump* that vibrated through Urya's paw pads. She observed them, a silent, silver-grey shadow at the edge of their flickering torchlight.

The Master, William Miller, walked at the front, his scent a sharp mix of gun oil, determination, and that familiar, challenging curiosity. Beside him, the farmer whose cattle had been eaten, his smell thick with righteous anger and grief, clutched a double-barreled shotgun, its metal glinting menacingly in the shifting light.

Other men carried lever-action rifles, their long barrels dark against the night sky, smelling of wood and cold steel. Some hefted axes, their sharpened blades catching the torch glow, smelling of fresh-cut timber and raw iron. A few gripped pitchforks, their tines like skeletal fingers, smelling of hay and desperate resolve.

They were a strange, formidable pack, their faces grim, their voices low purrs of resolve. Urya felt a strange surge of pride for these oblivious creatures. They were so obviously walking toward something that could, and would, kill them, yet they marched on. *They are so foolishly brave*, she thought, a detached amusement mixing with a flicker of concern. So easily fooled by their own loud sounds and clumsy plans.

The pride of humans followed the boy's frantic scent trail, a path of fear and rabbit blood, until they reached a watery dead end. The air here was colder, heavy with the scent of moving water, the deep, constant murmur of the Buffalo River filling the night. The river was wide, dark, and indifferent, its surface reflecting only the bruised, inky sky. The Gowrow's musky scent was strong here, a thick, cloying presence that made Urya's whiskers twitch with unease.

The humans stopped, their loud purrs turning into frustrated spits and sharp, questioning barks.

"It went in the water! We'll never find it in this dark!" a voice, smelling of stale fear, whined, advocating retreat. "Let's come back tomorrow, in the light! We'll drag the river then!"

"No! It's eaten enough! We go in now! Drag it out!" another voice, thick with rage and the sharp tang of cheap whiskey, snarled. This human smelled of raw, unthinking aggression, ready to plunge into the cold, dark water.

Others scattered, their scents spreading thin, moving along the riverbank, sniffing at the damp earth, searching for any other sign, any other path. They were like clumsy, two-legged dogs, sniffing without true purpose.

Then, the young boy, the one who had brought the rabbits, his scent still a mix of youthful fear and the metallic tang of fresh blood, moved toward a cluster of enormous boulders and ancient, rotten pine carcasses near the river's edge. He was small, his scent less confident than the adults, but his movements were precise, driven by a desperate need to prove himself.

He squeezed through a narrow gap between the rocks, his small body disappearing. A moment later, his voice, high-pitched and reedy, vibrated with a frantic energy. "Here! Over here! A cave! It's hidden behind these rocks!"

The humans converged, their scents of excitement and renewed purpose momentarily overpowering their fear.

"Clear it! Clear the way!" William Miller's voice boomed, sharp with command.

The sounds of heavy grunts, the scrape of boots against stone, the splintering of old wood filled the air as the men began to heave at the ancient debris, trying to expose the cave entrance.

# UNDERFOOT OF THE GOWROW

Urya flattened herself, her fur bristling. The Gowrow's smell was overwhelming now, thick and cold, emanating from the disturbed cave mouth. This was a mistake. A terrible, loud, clumsy mistake.

Suddenly, a massive, scaly form erupted from the disturbed water near the cave entrance. It was a blur of dark green and brown, moving with impossible speed. A flash of enormous tusks, a glimpse of a gaping maw.

The Gowrow, her scales slick with river water, lunged. There was a sickening thump, a strangled gurgle, and the boy's scent, sharp with terror, vanished beneath the churning surface of the river.

The Gowrow, with a silent, powerful surge, pulled him under, disappearing as quickly as she had appeared, leaving only disturbed water and the horrified, choked gasps of the humans.

Urya's fur stood on end. The humans were screaming now, a cacophony of fear and rage, their scents thick and overwhelming. The hunt had begun, but not in the way they had planned.

**Underfoot of a Legacy**
*Ozark Wilderness, Arkansas*
*October 23rd, 1897, 10:23 PM*

The Gowrow used her powerful, web-tipped limbs to pull her prey into the underwater causeways of the cave, dragging it swiftly into her bone-decorated lair. With the squirming boy clutched firmly in her massive jaws, she burst from beneath the surface of the cold, dark water. With a mighty fling of her head, she slung the boy onto a pile of deer and human bones, a fresh addition to her gruesome collection.

Underfoot, like a prayer no one had prayed, a furred savior hell-bent killing her new foe, now emerged. She had followed the beast through the chilling water, her fur slick, her small body trembling with cold and fury.

This was perfect, Urya thought, her mind a laser focus of predatory intent. While the monstrous thing was busy eating the child, she could kill, perhaps even eat it if she felt like it. The thought of the Gowrow's musky, reptilian flesh was repulsive, but the satisfaction of the kill, the ultimate dominance, was intoxicating.

The Gowrow's thoughts, however, countered this kitten-like fantasy with a swift, brutal slash of her scythe-like tail. The blade, as sharp as the knives in Mrs. Miller's kitchen, and as fast as Urya's own claws, whistled through the air. A bone-like edge slashed across Urya's fur, grazing her skin.

The creature had made her bleed her own blood.

This would end now.

Urya hissed, a sound of pure, unadulterated rage. The pain was a hot spark, igniting a deeper, primal fury. This giant, clumsy beast had dared to ignore her. It had dared to wound her. She launched herself again, a grey streak, not at the Gowrow's massive body, but directly at its head, aiming for the dark, ancient eyes. Her claws raked across the thick scales around one eye, a searing pain for the Gowrow, a desperate, satisfying tearing for Urya.

The Gowrow shrieked, a sound of pure agony, a high-pitched, piercing screech that was a twisted echo of her deep roar. She thrashed, her enormous head whipping back and forth, trying to dislodge the tiny, furious attacker. Urya clung on, digging her claws deeper, twisting, trying to find purchase on the slick, armored hide.

The Gowrow slammed against the cave wall, sending tremors through the rock, trying to crush the nuisance. Urya leaped, narrowly avoiding being flattened, landing lightly on a slippery pile of bones.

The Gowrow, momentarily disoriented, turned back to the boy, a new wave of hunger overriding her irritation. She lunged, her massive jaws opening, ready to claim her meal.

But Urya was faster.

With a furious, low growl, she darted between the Gowrow's legs, a silver streak, distracting it, drawing its attention away from the child.

She wasn't saving the boy; she was reclaiming her hunt. This was her prey, her challenge.

Suddenly, the cave entrance, still partially blocked by debris, was illuminated by a flickering, orange glow. The sound of heavy footsteps, splashing through the cold water, echoed through the cavern.

The humans were here. Up to their waists in the icy water, they held their lanterns high above their heads, their weapons clutched tight. Their scents—fear, gun oil, desperation—filled the air.

"There! There it is!" William Miller's voice boomed, a mixture of terror and triumph.

A flash of orange light.

A deafening *BOOM*.

The cave reverberated with the sound.

The Gowrow shrieked—a new, visceral note of agony—a wet, gurgling sound. The air filled with the acrid scent of gunpowder and the metallic tang of fresh, hot blood. The Gowrow stumbled—a massive, wounded hulk. Urya, caught in the concussion of the blast, was thrown against the cave wall, narrowly missing being hit by the scattered buckshot.

The Gowrow, gravely maimed hulk, turned and plunged deeper into the labyrinthine darkness of her cave, a desperate, wounded roar echoing behind her.

Urya, shaking off the impact, her fur bristling with renewed purpose, followed.

This was her kill.

She found the Gowrow in a narrow, water-filled passage, its immense body wedged between jagged rocks. Its breath came in ragged, wheezing gasps, its glowing eyes dimming.

Urya approached, silent, a tiny, determined shadow. She looked into those ancient, dying eyes. There was no fear, no anger, only a profound, weary acceptance. The Gowrow had lived a long, brutal life, and now it was over.

Urya met its gaze, a silent acknowledgment of the hunt, the struggle, the inevitable end. It was a final, shared moment between predator and predator.

Then, with a quiet, almost respectful finality, Urya delivered a swift, precise bite to the Gowrow's throat, severing the last thread of its ancient life.

The massive body shuddered, then fell still, sinking slightly into the murky water.

The humans, led by William Miller, soon found her. Their loud, triumphant shouts filled the cave as they dragged the Gowrow's immense carcass from the water, their faces grimed with mud and exhilaration.

More importantly, they quickly located the injured boy, who, though shaken and bruised, was alive and would survive to tell his father, a prominent local newspaper author, about the harrowing event. This incredible news story would first electrify the local newspaper and later be immortalized in folklore books.

They would celebrate, tell tales, and claim victory.

Urya, however, ignored their clumsy revelry. Her whiskers twitched, picking up a faint, intriguing scent from a hidden crevice near the back of the Gowrow's lair. She pushed past a pile of ancient bones, her keen eyes piercing the gloom. There, half-buried in the tough, damp soil, was a clutch of leathery, reptilian eggs, still warm. One, smaller than the rest, had a tiny crack, a faint vibration within.

Urya nudged the cracked egg with her nose, a strange curiosity overriding her usual predatory instincts. The vibration intensified, a faint tremor against her sensitive whiskers.

This wasn't prey. This was something new, something fragile, a life on the cusp of beginning. She looked back at the retreating humans, their triumphant shouts fading as they hauled the Gowrow's body away. They had claimed the kill, but they had missed the true legacy.

A low, guttural chirp came from the egg, a sound that resonated deep within Urya, a primal call she couldn't ignore.

# UNDERFOOT OF THE GOWROW

She pawed at the soil, carefully unearthing the small, quivering egg. It was an anomaly, a secret, a testament to the Gowrow's enduring presence in this forgotten corner of the world.

Urya, the hunter, the survivor, made a decision. This wasn't a meal. This was a responsibility. With the tiny, vibrating egg clutched gently in her jaws, she turned and disappeared into the deeper, uncharted darkness of the cave, leaving the humans to their fleeting triumph, and carrying the future of the Gowrow underfoot.

# THE SPRING

# ZACK GRAHAM

The sun was high when they reached Hatter's Creek, Population 63. Lance guided the car off the road and into the dusty lot of the service station. The place was small enough it didn't appear on the roadmap in Shannon's lap, yet here it stood, the first backwater township on the fringes of Mark Twain National Park.

The plan was to gas up, restock the snack bag, and press on into the wilderness.

Problem was, there was no one around; the street, the service station, the store—each more barren than the last. Lance putzed back and forth between the aisles, certain something was wrong.

"I'm telling you, this is weird," he said. "Where is everybody?"

"It's small-town life, babe. They probably closed for lunch—or church," Shannon said, looking over a rack of packaged pastries.

"Well, I'm done waiting. Let's get in the car and hit the road before we lose any more daylight."

"It's the longest day of the year. I think we have plenty of time," Shannon said.

It was true. This whole trip was planned around the Summer Solstice.

The front door chimed open before Lance could respond, and he turned to find a kid sneaking through the opening. They both froze, exchanging a universal look: *what the hell are you doing here?*

The kid turned and started to run back out the door.

"Hey, wait!" Lance nearly shouted. "You live here?"

The kid stopped and nodded. He couldn't have been older than ten.

"We're from O'Fallon, just driving through to Piney Creek. Do you know where that is?"

The boy nodded and said something, but Lance couldn't understand him.

"Can you tell us where everyone is?" he tried asking instead.

"Dey down yonder, by the water, like dey do," he said.

Lance and Shannon shared a look.

"Will they be coming back soon?" Lance pressed.

"Hard t'say," the boy said with a shrug. "They wen' down t'kiss the spring on account'a the solstice."

"Kiss the spring?" Lance echoed.

"Yup," the boy said, waving a hand for them to follow. "This way."

The trio exited the building and walked around back, where an old limestone staircase cut through the bushes. The steps looked ancient, laid right into the hillside. The boy led them down through a dogwood canopy where the air felt much cooler.

They heard water next, and soon, people clamoring somewhere in the distance. The foliage was too dense to see through, but after rounding the last bend, the hickory and cedar opened into a beautiful

# THE SPRING

cove along a river. Folks stood in a loose ring around a rocky opening where the water pushed out of the hillside and into the pool below.

There was an old wooden sign pegged to a tree. It read SUN SPRING.

"Nice swimming hole," Shannon said.

The boy looked up at her and shook his head.

"We don' dip a toe in that water," he mumbled. "Only t'day."

"Why not?" Lance scoffed.

"It belong to the Sun," was all the boy said.

A man closer to the river turned back to look at them. He had thin, combed hair and a collared shirt tucked into a pair of faded blue jeans. He smiled, nodded, and stepped up the hillside.

"Where'd you go, Clive? Better not be stealin' all my candy from the store, boy," the older man said to the kid.

"I wasn't, Mr. Kirby," Clive said, pointing to Lance and Shannon. "They were waitin' at the station."

The man nodded and turned an eye on the couple.

"Good morning," Lance offered. "The kid said we'd find you all down here."

"Yep, come down for the solstice. Should be done soon, then I'll getcha taken care of," he said, turning back to face the water. Clive walked near a spot where the cliff dropped off and peered into the churning depths below.

Lance and Shannon settled into the background as they watched the celebration. Those standing nearest the spring seemed to be chanting a hymn of some kind, while all the others stood with their eyes closed and their mouths open, reaching their palms toward the sky.

"Well, it looks like this is a bust," Lance said, nodding up the stairwell. "Let's get back to the car and get out of here."

"No, wait," Shannon said, looking over his shoulder. "Look at that."

She raised a finger toward the spring.

Lance slowly turned.

What had been a gorgeous flowing faucet was now stopped up with a big, spongy cork of some kind. He would've thought it was rock, except it had the fluid movements of a lung, slowly expanding outward before pulling back into the rubble of the spring. Lance watched it balloon out several times as the locals lined up beside it.

He took a step toward Mr. Kirby, who hadn't joined the congregation.

"What is it?" Lance asked the old man.

"The solstice ceremony," Mr. Kirby answered.

"No, what is *that?*" Lance clarified, pointing a finger at the wheezing membrane.

"Oh," Kirby laughed. "We don't know."

They looked over just as the first few worshipers leaned over and placed their lips against the tissue. They delivered a single kiss, ducked under the balloon as it filled up, and then jumped into the water below.

Lance looked back to Shannon in horror.

*They go down t'kiss the spring...*

This was what the kid was talking about. Lance scampered up the hill and pulled Shannon after him.

"What's going on?"

"We need to get the hell out of here," Lance said. "This. Is. Crazy."

"What? It's just some hick tradition—"

"No, that thing is fucking alive, do you hear me?"

Lance could hear more people jumping into the water as they argued. And then he heard them scream.

Their words hitched and they both turned back to the creek. The only folks they could see were the boy and Mr. Kirby. The boy stood vacant, while the older man clapped and cheered at the procession. Lance took Shannon's hand and together they crept back up the stairs.

Most of the locals had already kissed the thing and jumped into the pool, but there were twenty or thirty still in line. The screams came from the others, swimming down below. The couple watched as, one by one,

# THE SPRING

something yanked them under the surface, and not a single person returned.

Above them all, the membrane expanded much more frantically, turning from a balloon into a sail. It extended above the rocks, above the trees, until the end of it popped loose and exposed it for what it was.

It wasn't a lung or wad of subterranean protein; it was the first great arm of a starfish, stuck in the fresh mountain spring. It wasn't the spines along the top or tubes along the bottom that gave it away, it was the four other arms spread out beneath the water. The pool proved so crystal clear, Lance could see its unmistakable body sprawling across the creek floor.

He watched as the arms snaked up to the surface and yanked the locals under.

*We don' dip a toe in that water...*

It was obvious why. The spring had additional openings underneath, where the starfish could push the rest of its body through. For whatever reason, it forced its head up through the waterfall, where a beady little eye looked down at the folks kissing it.

*It belong to the Sun.*

The creature spread out symmetrically for a moment, and Lance saw it indeed looked like a child's drawing of a sun. He crept closer to Clive and tugged on the boy's sleeve, careful not to get Kirby's attention.

"Where are your parents?" Lance asked.

The boy pointed down toward the spring.

"Are they in line or in the water?"

"They got took last summer," the boy said, on the verge of tears.

Lance wondered what kind of godless community fed parents to the river and left the children alone. His eyes landed on Clive and Lance decided he couldn't leave the boy. Not with these people.

He grabbed Clive by the shoulder and ushered him toward Shannon. The trio ascended the stairs together, just as they came down.

Behind them, the population of Hatter's Creek continued to scream.

"What the hell was all that?" Shannon asked as they climbed the last step.

Lance didn't respond.

"Where we goin'?" Clive asked.

"We're leaving. We're getting you out of here," Shannon explained. "Don't worry about anything."

They came upon the car and stopped. All four of the tires were punctured and deflated. A sick, liquid worry started to fill Lance's stomach.

"Come on now, boy!" Mr. Kirby hollered from down the stairwell. "Let's go take a swim!"

"Get inside," Lance said, ushering the others toward the service station.

Clive didn't hesitate to enter. Shannon stood on the exterior porch, looking into the dingy country store as if it were the inside of a wound. Lance came jogging up behind her, and with a gentle push, guided her through the door frame.

He turned and secured the latch, which barely hooked the rickety door in place.

"We gotta block this door," he said to himself.

"Mr. Kirby keeps a hammer and nails in the backroom," Clive offered.

Lance nodded, scanning the main floor for anything else he could use. His eyes glanced over a wall of glass soda bottles behind two double doors.

"Help me," he said.

It was a large standing cooler that was more than twice the size of the door; plenty to block up the entrance. Lance gripped the closest side and put everything he had into cavemanning the unit over, while Shannon and Clive struggled to push it from the other side. The trio slowly muscled the cooler until it filled the frame.

"Go get the hammer," Lance said.

"But the soda—" the boy started.

"Just go get the hammer!"

Clive scrambled off into another room.

Shannon ran her hands through her hair; all the color had bled from her face.

"What are we going to do?" she asked.

*Protect you.*

"I don't know," Lance said. "We have to get out of here."

"How?"

*Whatever it takes.*

"Hey! Mister!" Clive screamed from the back.

Something slammed into the side of the building.

Lance and Shannon shared a momentary look of disbelief.

He moved first, but they both dashed into the next room. Lance turned the corner to find a dusty old storage area, and at the back of it, Clive stood with both hands pressed against a shaking back door.

"Open the fuckin' door, you little shit!" Kirby barked through the wall.

The boy whimpered in response but pushed even harder against the flimsy wood.

"Where's the hammer, kid?" Lance asked.

Shannon bolted to the door and helped Clive keep it shut.

"You're strong for a little cotton hair," Kirby roared. "*Now open. The DOOR!*"

He smashed into the wood so hard it began to crack right down the middle. Both Clive and Shannon cried beneath the impacts, watching in horror as the entire door folded in two.

Lance went from table to table, shuffling piles of receipts and inventory sheets, desperate for the weight of the hammer in his hands. Defeated, he gave up the tabletops and took a peek below, where he discovered dozens of milk crates filled with all manner of odds and ends.

While he searched, the sounds of Kirby's threats spilled in through the door. They were hard to make out, especially over the whimpers of Shannon and the boy.

A rage came to life just under Lance's skin, a prehistoric hate handed down from a longline of survivors. Brutes. Lance's eyelids peeled back enough for his eyes to bulge, and there, hanging from a wall hook, he spotted the hammer.

It filled the space in his palm as if it were made for him.

"Help us!" Shannon screamed.

Lance turned to see Mr. Kirby's fingers sliding in through the crack.

"Ya'll owe me for the door," he said. "Now, OPEN UP!"

"Move," Lance said.

Both Shannon and Clive looked back, but neither stepped out of the way.

Lance showed them the hammer.

"Let him in," he said as evenly as he could.

Shannon went silent and peeled herself away from the door, but it took Clive a little longer to quit pushing back.

The little boy jumped to the side and let the boards fall inward.

"'Bout time, letting me into my own *goddamn* store," he muttered as he climbed through the crack he made. Shannon took Clive in her arms and backpedaled.

"Yeah, you better—" Kirby started. He stopped when he spotted Lance and the hammer.

"Oh."

"Yeah," Lance confirmed.

Kirby opened his mouth, but he didn't get the chance to speak. Lance lunged forward like a silverback, all shoulders and arms, as he windmilled the hammerhead into Kirby's eyes, teeth, and nose. The shopkeeper brought his hands up to stop the blows, but it was too late; Lance cracked him once more in the brow and Kirby fell back, tumbling down the hillside.

Lance stepped out into the woodland, scanning for more townies.

Slowly, Shannon and the boy came out to join him.

"Where'd he go?" Shannon asked.

Lance just pointed down the slope with the bloodied end of the hammer.

"Is anyone else coming?" Shannon asked.

Lance turned to Clive.

"Is there somewhere nearby? Anywhere to hide?"

The boy shook his head.

"Nowhere safe," he said through gapped teeth.

"What about a truck? Or a phone?" Lance pressed. "Does anyone have electricity in this shithole?"

Clive shook his head. His eyes fluttered around the trees like he was following a bird.

"He's shellshocked, kid's useless—" Lance started.

"The Bybells have a truck," Clive said. "They haul oats 'n hay with it."

"Where?"

Clive beckoned and started into the forest.

They went single file down what appeared to be a game trail. A nearly vertical slope led down to the spring on their right, uninterrupted trees to their left. Lance was grateful. They wouldn't have survived their initial descent to the creek without the kid.

Someone screamed from the forest behind them. Other voices joined in.

They jogged along the trail as quick as the terrain allowed; one misstep would send them plummeting to almost certain death… if not, a plunge into the crystal-clear spring below, which Lance considered just as fatal.

Something cracked a tree to his left, and it took Lance a moment to realize it was a bullet. His ears rang so loud he couldn't hear Shannon screaming. It wasn't until the second report came, and the fire erupted through his arm, that everything came together.

All he could do was scream.

"Run!" Shannon said, bolting with Clive into the trees.

Lance sprang after them, turning to see who was shooting. He could see a gnarled face peeking up from the barrel, fixed between the split trunk of an oak tree. Kirby's swollen, bloodied features were unmistakable.

"Go on, boy! Bring me that *HIDE!*" he screamed through the branches.

Lance shook his head. *Boy?*

Something else moved on the other side of the trail, along the steep face of the slope. Lance thought it was a deer at first, but as it scrambled nearer, he could plainly see it was a man, scrawny and naked, tearing through the leaves. He moved like a mountain goat, sure-footed and wiry.

Lance turned but it was no use. The goat-man shot by and disappeared in the foliage.

Shannon screamed a second later.

"What the *fuck,*" Lance breathed, tearing off through the brush. Kirby fired another round, and it whistled off into the thicket too.

There wasn't time to deal with the shopkeeper again; Lance wasn't prepared to deal with a rifle. He zigzagged between the trunks until he caught sight of Shannon.

The naked man had her pinned to the ground, Clive pulling uselessly at his back. It was hard to focus on; not because of the chaos, or the disbelief he held in his heart, but because there was a building just beyond the clearing. Building besides, there was *a truck,* an actual vehicle in this dump of a town.

Shannon screamed for help.

She pushed with her hands, her feet, but it was no use. The guy was *strong,* teeth snapping right in her face. He was pale and hairless, reminding Lance of an albino. Whatever he was, he was proving to be a serious issue.

Behind him, somewhere in the woods, Kirby reloaded his rifle.

# THE SPRING

Shannon fought with everything she had, but it didn't matter. The thing on top of her muscled her arms against the ground, bruised her thighs as it pushed her flat. She tried to buck with her hips and torso, but that only allowed the creature to wrap one of its legs around her. Rancid froth dribbled down from its gnashing teeth.

She screamed bloody horror.

Clive was somewhere close. Shannon couldn't see him, but she could hear his strained breathing. They both worked to upend the pale, pasty man on top of her, but the more they struggled, the more purchase he found. His teeth would find her neck at any moment.

And then something shot out of the forest, connected with the goat-man, and both of them fell over to Shannon's left. She thought it was a young bull or an elk, but when she rolled over to get up, she could see the faded T-shirt and jeans; it was Lance, red faced, veins bursting to life along his neck as he wrestled for top position. Blood ran freely from a gash in his arm.

Shannon started to crawl toward him, but Clive yanked her away.

"No, no!" he screamed. "He'll kill you! Come on!"

She looked down and knew he was telling the truth. There was something off about that pale, emaciated body. Why the hell was he strong? She let Clive yank her toward the farmhouse while she tried to reason.

A thud brought the scuffle to a momentary pause. Somehow Lance still had grip of the hammer, and he brought it up alongside the goat-man's head. The creature went stiff and toppled over, but only long enough for Lance to stand up. The pasty thing shook off the fog and got ready to pounce.

Lance brought the hammer up and almost looked like he was smiling.

Another report flattened the area, and Lance was the only one to move. He stumbled sideways as fresh ribbons of blood stained the belly of his shirt. Kirby came stalking out of the trees with his rifle a moment later.

"Come *on*," Clive said, still pulling on her. "It's over, we gotta *go!*"

Shannon was powerless, her eyes steaming with fresh tears as her boyfriend collapsed to the earth without a sound.

The goat-man was on him then, pulling off his ears and eating them like jerky.

Her only hope was to run.

She fell in line behind Clive before overtaking him. Shannon beat him to the truck and hopped in the driver's seat, frantically looking around for the key. The boy ran around the far side and squeezed in himself, slapping both locks with the flat of his palms.

"There's no key!" she said.

"There," Clive said, pointing a finger into the ashtray.

A single flake of silver gleamed back.

She fingered it out of the tar and jammed it in the ignition.

Shannon looked up from the wheel to the windshield, and to her horror found Kirby smiling back at her. He was a blur, as Shannon's main focus was the black portal of the barrel leveled right at her chest. The goat-man paced on all fours in front of Kirby.

"Go on, now," he said. "Get outta the—"

Lance didn't let him finish.

Earless, punched through with bullet holes, he rose to his feet and arced the hammer into the back of Kirby's head. The battered hick smashed face-first into the ground and then began to twitch.

Shannon screamed, "Get in the truck! Get over here!"

She laid on the horn just to make sure.

"You gotta start it first!" Clive said.

She realized it wasn't on. After coaxing the pedal and cranking the ignition a few times, Shannon got the engine to catch. It roared to life with a spat of black smoke.

# THE SPRING

Kirby continued to convulse, no longer a threat; it was the goat-man everyone was watching. It thrashed and howled, running back and forth as it looked over its wounded papa. It wanted to attack Lance again, but he showed too much grit, too much life and blood. There seemed to be a bizarre, animalistic respect between them.

Shannon saw all the pieces in motion and shifted the truck into drive, punched the gas, and guided the squirrely wheel right at the naked bastard. She and Clive both braced for the impact.

The grill caught him flush across the shoulders, and the old knobby tires chewed the body right under the frame. The creature didn't howl, only whimpered like a baby as it was crushed to a puddle beneath the weight.

Shannon didn't let off the gas until she was even with Lance, at which point she jumped from the cab and helped him to his feet.

"We're getting you out of here, baby," Shannon said.

They were both covered in his blood after just a couple steps. It pulsed from him like a broken pipe.

"It's okay, I'm okay," Lance said as he eased himself into the truck bed. "We gotta call 911."

Shannon looked at the cavern in his belly as she slapped the tailgate shut.

"We'll get help. Keep pressure on it, don't fall asleep," she said.

She found Clive sitting in the same spot down the bench seat. Her faith in the engine wavered as she pulled the door closed and punched the gas. It hesitated but eventually chugged forward.

Shannon drove as fast as she could. With all the turns, and Lance free to slide around in the back, she had to keep it steady. Clive peered over the seat back and into the truck bed.

"He ain't gonn' make it."

"Where can we take him? Is there a hospital?"

"Over in Rolla. That's what I'm sayin', he ain't gonna make it," Clive said again.

"There has to be something here, a doctor, a first-aid kit—"

"They don't use medicine here. The spring is the only remedy."

"*Shut up!*" Shannon screamed at the top of her lungs.

Clive didn't recoil, just sat back in the seat and rested an elbow against the dingy metal door.

"We all drink the water; we don't get sick. If someone get hurt, we soak it in the spring and it's healed over and strong by morning," the boy said. "It'll even make ya young."

The road straightened out, and up ahead, Shannon spotted the service station and the rest of town as it careened into view.

She glanced at Clive; he smiled back at her, and for just a moment, he looked like someone else.

"What are you talking about? Younger?"

"Just what I said," came the answer.

Lance groaned from the bed. Shannon looked over her shoulder and found she could no longer see the grooves of the metal. It was filled with an inch of sloshing blood.

"Oh, God."

"He need the water."

"God dammit, shut up!" Shannon screamed.

Clive chuckled.

"You sound jus' like my son."

She glanced at him again, that same alien look.

"Son?"

"Yeah, my son. Kirby," Clive said, nodding over his shoulder. "It's him that the boy, ain't me."

He winked.

Shannon went nuclear.

"You're a kid—what are you talking about?"

"Only 'cause it was my turn to be young," he answered, puckering his lips. "Someone gotta run the station."

Before she could respond, Clive launched himself across the bench seat, gripped the wheel, and jerked it to the left. They fought for control,

# THE SPRING

but the sudden shift sent the truck rolling off the dusty old road, through the trees, and down the slope.

They were suddenly rocketing toward the creek. They passed behind the back of the station again, even cut near the same limestone staircase, before the bed racked a tree and sent the whole machine spinning the other direction. Shannon prayed they connected with a few more to prevent them from going in the water.

Clive let go of the wheel and grabbed onto her, and his face was that of a wild animal. He climbed Shannon's form like a rabid monkey, until his hands were wrapped around her face, fingers pressing into her eyes.

Before she could fight him off, the truck left the earth and they were in a freefall. Shannon's guts floated between her lungs and up into her throat.

The truck impacted and wasted no time sinking. Water flooded in through rusted holes in the floorboards, and Shannon was up to her knees in cool ripples in less than five seconds.

She tried to look in the bed, but Clive was blocking her vision.

"Drink up," he said. "Drink deep."

Shannon screamed, driving her elbow backward one, two, three times, connecting right with the little shit's head. She heard it bounce off the rusted metal of the cab on the other side.

Leaning back, now she could see into the bed, where fresh spring water mixed with the blood and made a strange, beautiful concoction. Lance floated in the fluid, eyes fighting to stay fixed on something. His face was white like snow.

The back window had a sliding panel, which she threw open and scampered through one excruciating inch at a time. The narrow frame bruised her ribs and back as she fought her way through. By the time Shannon fell into the bed, the entire truck was underwater, only bubbles and blood escaping the metal tomb. Clive sank away from the surface without a sound.

Shannon did her best to keep Lance afloat, using one arm to hold his head, and the rest of her limbs kicking for dear life. Using the natural current of the creek, she did her best to guide them to shore.

Up above, along the tree lines, children appeared out of the bushes. They watched with an indifferent stare.

"Hey!" Shannon yelled. "Down here! Help us!"

None of them moved.

She figured they were like Clive, hiding in town… until she saw they were all dripping wet.

They were the same locals that came down to kiss the spring, the folks that jumped into the pool.

They were young now. Children.

She remembered the membrane escaping the spring.

Shannon realized the creature's appendage wasn't hanging out of the rock slot. Ice traced up from the very tips of her toes; it could only be beneath them. She imagined the truck coming down to disturb its delicate lair.

Lance sputtered in and out of consciousness in her arms. Every breath was half muddled with creek water. Exhaustion crept into Shannon's heart, and the weight of reality told her their fate.

Something tickled the bottom of her foot, and before she could pull away, it took hold. Spongy yet rigid, Shannon had never felt such a sensation; soft like watermoss but framed inside with bones. Every part of her wanted to panic, to kick with all her might… but there was something welcoming about the touch. It was delicate, considerate, and almost seemed to push her up to tread water. Shannon kept afloat but she dared not look down.

"It's alright," she found herself saying into Lance's waterlogged ear.

Gently, it began to pull. Shannon felt the muscles and bones in her leg straighten and align, even pop where needed, and then her head was underwater. The current moved only in one direction, away from the spring, but she could feel motion all around her. Curtains of flesh and membrane gliding through the water. She wondered if Clive had felt the same sensations when he drowned at the bottom of the pool.

She held onto Lance's hand, and slowly they sank lower and lower, until only darkness waited beyond her eyelids.

When Shannon was able to take a breath again, she didn't know how much time had passed. Minutes, days, weeks; none of that had any meaning. Only the fresh forest air filling her lungs mattered.

Shannon opened her eyes and found herself treading water. She floated near shore, and the sun was almost gone.

Lance bobbed in the water too, just ahead of her.

She was shocked when he turned to face her. No beard, no wrinkles. He was just a kid.

Shannon looked down at her little hands and screamed.

# THE APPLE AND THE TREE

## RICHARD BEAUCHAMP

As those old, rolling green hills rose up from the horizon like some verdant ocean, dread burned a cold hole in my stomach. Under different circumstances, the sight of those regal domed mountains rising up from the alluvial flats of my other life would bring joy. The Ozarks were my birthright, my home. But this time I was being called home to help salt an old wound.

You can't deny blood. When word came that my mama had gone missin' up in the Saint Francois range, my veins sung with it. The song of family. The song of loyalty.

# RICHARD BEAUCHAMP

Scoot, my trusty coon dog, shot up from his position riding shotgun in my old Tacoma as Route 72 began to snake and slalom its way up to the high country. Scoot, like the rest of the dogs on our farm down in Malden, had only ever known the tabletop flatlands of the bootheel. His beagle snout knew the tang of manure, the mephitic aroma of the Miss leaving behind her stagnant floodwater as a fertile tithe, and pesticides from the miles of farmland that was our home.

Now I had to wonder what he smelled as we drove through Bollinger and into Madison County, and the swampy bottoms gave way to hard, stony soil and pine forest, and the mountains took shape ahead like god's green molars, occluding the horizon.

The old family stead was located on the county line between Madison and Iron Counties, in a little township you've never heard of called New Hamlin. The Hensley demesne was a humble two-story Victorian house that had long gone to seed with creeper vine inching up its once-eggshell-white walls, now stained a greenish patina from time and neglect.

My mother was never one for vanity. While most middle-aged women out here in the hills were busy reading *Better Homes & Gardens*, and waiting for their men to get home from their shifts at the lead mines, my mother was slapping pulpy poultices over infected cuts, brewing teas from local flora to help women with the cramps of their monthlies, and, more often than not, helping settle the balance between this world and that of the beyond.

You see, my mother was what us hill folk call a grannywoman. The appellations may differ slightly depending on where you're at. Appalachia might call her a mountain witch. Here in the Ozarks, the term goober doctor or power doctor might apply. But *Grannywoman* is what most called her, even if her services sometimes went beyond mere herbalism and rustic mountain medicine.

I turned off 72, onto County Road 308. The Tacoma's worn suspension groaned and protested as I drove carefully over the many washouts and potholes, stands of white oak and poplar hemming in the road on either side, the branches interlocking above to give the illusion of going down some vast sylvan tunnel.

I felt my heart start to stutter in my chest as we rounded a rise and the homestead came into view. The yard was grown up waist high. A gaggle of raccoons exploded out from under my old man's rust-eaten 1500 that sat on cinderblocks beside the driveway, the weeds eager to reclaim the truck.

"Well boy, whatchu think?" I asked Scoot, who gave me the conflicting doggy messages of a waggy tail and cocked back ears. Scoot didn't know what to think, and hell, I didn't either.

I got out and let Scoot sniff around while I tied my long red hair up in a bun and stretched my legs. It was a two-hour drive from my daddy's farm down in Malden, but it felt like a hundred as his words filled my soul with a potato sack worth of guilt.

*Never mind what sort of mess that witch momma of yours got into. You don't need to get involved. Hell, that's the whole reason I moved us down here to the swamps*, he'd said as I got in my truck. When he saw I was serious, he became a bit more desperate. *You know she's fallen far from God, Essy. You know—*

That's when I'd cut him off and started up the truck. The bootheel is God's country alright, and my daddy was of the Baptist flavor.

I went to church for a while, just because it got me out of farm work on Sundays, until I got older, that is, and figured out why it was my gaze kept falling on the preacher's daughter instead of the broad shoulders of the farm hands we hired every harvest season. *Jesus don't kin to queers, honey, but I love you all the same*, Daddy had said.

Not really sure what I was supposed to make of that, but my daddy tried his best to raise me normal-like. When my momma understood I had the 'seein''-blood' as she called it, my trials as her protégé began before I even knew what 'menstruation' was. When Daddy saw what she was doing, boy, he got mad.

# RICHARD BEAUCHAMP

You see, my momma didn't just settle upset tummies and make fertility charms for couples trying for a family. She could also see things others couldn't.

For lack of a better word, *exorcist* is something that might be applied to my mother's long resume of backwoods duties. Although, put out of your mind scenes of a preacher fella saying the Lord's Prayer over some peaked individual speaking in tongues and spoutin' blaspheme.

Nah, see, what most people don't understand is hauntings ain't just a human affair. Nor a godly one. See, these hills up here is *old*. Older even than our Smokie cousins to the east.

And when you got land like this, that's been unchanged for billions of years, with its many labyrinthine caverns and verdant vitality, certain things tend to settle down there. Sometimes they're beings, entities who've been a part of the land ever since these mountains were under water and spoutin' lava.

Other times it's just an… hell, I guess *energy* is the word I'd use. A miasmal haze that clings to the land, and affects the wildlife, the plants, and the people that dare inhabit it.

See, us humans and these ancient energies? We don't get along so good. Their very existence is inimical to ours. You'd know what I'm talking about if you ever walked through a place infested with it, a place that just doesn't "feel right." You'd start to feel real peculiar right quick.

And let's say you bought a parcel of land to live on that just so happens to have such unwanted indigenous features, well, after a few weeks that peaked feeling manifests into illness that'll plumb kill you after a spell.

Most people couldn't physically see these ephemeral blights, and hence where the misnomer of 'cursed land' forever cemented itself into hill folk superstition.

It was Momma's job to rid the hollers and hills of these pockets of the unknown. Because unlike most others, she could see it, these things that slipped through the fabric of the beyond.

And I could too.

Inside, the house was tidy, which in itself was a harbinger. My mother was what some today would call a hoarder, and not a very neat one at that. For her to focus her neurotic mind long enough to pick up after herself meant she was plannin' to face something she knew she might not come back from. And I had a pretty good idea what that something was.

As Scoot sniff-vestigated the rest of the house, I went back to my momma's study, which was a room filled with everything from jarred medicinal herbs she picked and grew in her backyard (which encompassed the mountain that loomed over the house) to various wooden sigils made out of pawpaw and ash wood (both being sacred timber species in these parts) dangling from the ceiling.

The roots of Queen Anne's Lace, mullein stalks, echinacea buds, and other medicinal herbs sat drying in a windowsill above one small desk. It was here where she hand wrote dosing instructions for each herb, or copied incantations from special grimoires written by old, old scholars who knew of such ephemeral blights that lurk in the darkness between trees and in the caves where no light ever shone.

It was on this desk I saw the neatly folded piece of stationary that simply read *Esther.*

I opened the letter, the paper trembling as I struggled to get a hold of myself.

*My dearest daughter—*
*If you're reading this, it's because you're here, in my house. I know that would only happen if news of my demise has reached you, and with how nosy folks are in New Hamlin, I'm sure that news reached you directly.*

## RICHARD BEAUCHAMP

*I'm sure you know what has happened to me, and where I've gone. But in case time, or perhaps all those nasty chemicals your daddy sprays on his crops, has fogged your mind, I'll state it plainly.*

*I've gone to Three Rivers to face the blight that lurks there. I know I always warned you to stay away from there, to never, ever try your skills with the abomination that lurks in that cave... But Essy, dear, the blight is spreading. I can ignore it no longer. Folks around New Hamlin have been talking about the animal mutilations... the big bare patch of dead forest that's been spreading north of town, the way that stretch of Castor River keeps spitting out dead bass and bream. I'm afraid if I don't do something about it, it'll spread until all of New Hamlin is consumed. There's already been talk of the Chism's, who have property on Three Rivers, falling deathly ill.*

*You'll find the tools you need beside this letter. You know what to do with them, Esther. It may have been many years since you last helped me cleanse a holler, but I know you remember.*

*I'm just an old woman now, and I doubt I'll have the energy or the spryness to rid the Three Rivers cave of that foul booger. I hope you finish what I started, Esther. I know your daddy tried his hardest to rid you of your mystic instincts. But... Well, you know what they say about the apple and the tree.*

*I love you, daughter of mine.*

*And I'm sorry to drag you into this.*

"Damnit..." I sighed as I leaned heavily against the desk, my spine suddenly feeling like it was made of Jell-o. Scoot rushed in and nudged my leg, no doubt sensing my distress.

"Oh, I'm fine, you silly mutt," I said as I knelt down to scratch his ears, but that was a damn lie. I was anything but, and getting worse as I looked at the other items on the desk.

The engraved spirit box, whose walls I knew were lined with ash wood and had a silver-plated bottom. And the piece of metal beside it that resembled a rail road spike. But it was no ordinary piece of pig iron,

# THE APPLE AND THE TREE

and as I picked it up, I felt it tingle in my hand. Pure ferro iron, with a silver core in its middle.

I sighed and looked toward the south wall, where a shelf stood. That shelf was filled with spirit boxes identical to the empty one on the table. Each one was locked shut with a silver band and lock. Each one had fine black wisps of smoke leaking out from the edges as if a mini tire fire blazed inside it. I knew no one else besides me, and maybe Scoot, could see the residual blight vapors.

I turned to Scoot, knelt, and cupped his face in my hands.

"What say you boy, you wanna go on an adventure?"

Scoot's a smart dog. Like the rest of the workin' dogs on our farm, he knows over twenty commands and has an intelligence that'd rival most mouth-breathing booger eaters you see at your local Wal-Mart. Scoot knew what adventure meant.

But most importantly, he knew how to track. He was the best damn tracker dog I'd ever had and had treed his share of coons and squirrels. Which was why I brought him along.

Before I left the house, I grabbed one of my momma's bandanas. One of the unwashed ones that was stiff and crinkly with her old sweat.

Three Rivers lies about four miles west of New Hamlin and is named such because of it being the confluence of, well, three rivers: the Saint Francis, the White Stone, and the Castor.

Once a popular floating spot for kayakers and canoers for its access to each river and the picturesque karst bluffs that dot the area, Three Rivers has since been abandoned due to the preternaturally high level of 'incidents' that occur.

These 'incidents' seemed to happen right around the point where the bluffs get especially tall, pocked with cave openings whose darkness refuses to dissipate even under a high noon sun.

## RICHARD BEAUCHAMP

Folks reported feeling faint and lightheaded around the river junctions. Others who would get out onto the banks to relieve themselves or fish would find themselves wandering the woods miles away, in a fugue and with no idea how they got there. Local fauna such as raccoons, coyotes, and deer were found at the base of the bluffs, their skulls caved in as if some demented soul had decided to go at them with a sledgehammer.

And now the fish were feeling it too, which was a damn shame. I used to catch *beaucoup* smallmouth and walleye in those streams. The blight had taken my mama *and* ruined my fishin' holes. You could say things were gettin' personal, now.

My momma knew of the blight at Three Rivers long before most others did. She'd been an avid archivist of local history and had learned of the 'Ozark Bluff-Dwellers,' as they were called, the proto-native Americans who came to our hills long before the Osage and Shawnee rolled through.

She'd learned through first-hand accounts of the anthropologists who came here to study native artifacts and instead found paintings in the many cavern systems that connected underneath these old mountains for many subterranean miles. Of the warnings they left on those sandstone walls depicting the shadowy horrors that were born from the deepest, most primordial depths of those stone gullets.

As I drove into town to get some supplies, I reflected on what Mama told me about those energies. About how if you left 'em to simmer, they'd grow, metastasize like the worst kind of cancer, and the longer you let 'em sit, the harder they was to excise.

I pulled into the local HARPS, kept the windows cracked for Scoot, and went in, praying time and physical maturity would render me anonymous to most of the New Hamlinites.

I shoulda known better.

Ain't many gingers in New Hamlin.

I went in and grabbed what I needed with haste: two big bottles of water, some high-calorie protein bars, triple A batteries for my headlamp, and some Milk-Bones for Scoot.

"My stars, is that Esther Hensley I see?" came a croaky old voice as I quickly ran my items through self-checkout. I bit back a visible cringe as I turned and saw Abraham Milton coming toward me with that wooden arthritic gait of his.

"Howdy, Abe, long time, no see," I said, knowing he'd hate that nickname. If you were a New Hamlin citizen, you knew him as *Reverend Abraham,* and he expected you to address him as such. He ran the First Baptist church down on Lordell Street and had one of the biggest congregations this side of the Saint Francis. But Reverend Abraham, godly man he claimed to be, was no stranger to slander and libel.

"I assume you come back 'cause of your mother. True shame that is. Heard she went plumb crazy and wandered off in the hills yonder. It was such a relief when I heard you and your daddy left all that heathen madness long ago. Farmin's good, Christian wo—"

"Abe—" I said, bagging my stuff and turning to meet the man's direct but somehow wounded gaze full on. "My momma once helped your daughter when she had the measles bad, had her drink up a tea of stinging nettle and calendula. This was after you kept her locked up in that house and let her rot as you 'prayed it away.' She recovered right quick, if I recall. After that you had the audacity to say my family was in league with the devil. You barred my daddy from your church. Did you think I forgot that?"

"Well, Esther, I—"

"I may be a farmer, Rev, but guess what? I'm grown now, and I'm as gay as the day is long. You hear that? *I date women.*" I punctuated those last three words with a provocative waggle of my eyebrows. "Now go spread some gossip about *that*, you ignorant old fart."

# RICHARD BEAUCHAMP

I got back to my truck without further molestation from other nosey town folk and started driving. Savoring the reverend's look of horrified shock.

Now, I mentioned these creek-side caverns. What I didn't mention was that they sit about fifty feet up on sheer rock walls. Some folks can scale them with mountain climbing equipment. I didn't have all that, nor the necessary water craft to get at them from that angle.

However, I knew of one entrance a mile or so away from Three Rivers one can hike up to enter. The problem was, it was on private property, and my memory of how to get there was a bit hazy. But that's where my Scoot came in.

Tom Allen was (and maybe still is) a fat, and rich, lawyer who owned most of the land around New Hamlin. A big spread that encompassed over forty acres just outside the eastern town limits.

Most of it was unused, but some of it he had cleared away for a deer hunting tract where he flew in his rich buddies from around the state to drink expensive whiskey and talk stock market hoodoo until a buck decided to come lick one of their salt blocks. Though most of the land was unused, he had game cameras setup every quarter mile, and God help you if you even strolled a foot past the designated property line.

But word spreads like bad gas in a high wind around places like New Hamlin, and I'd heard from my dad that Tom Allen was laid low with heart failure and hadn't left his big McMansion on McCallister hill in years. Which was good news for me, because Tom's land happened to contain the one easily accessible cavern entrance that, after a few underground twists and turns, would take you to the bluffs overlooking Three Rivers.

I didn't know where it was exactly, and Mama hadn't had the foresight to draw a map, but Scoot would lead me there, I was sure.

# THE APPLE AND THE TREE

I turned off a county road onto the start of Tom's property and began to meander the maze of steep dirt trails that crisscrossed his land, half expecting some private security team to come out of the bushes and ambush me.

Eventually I found an old 4x4 track where he drove those souped-up ATVs that probably had the spinning rims. It looked to head in the general direction I wanted to go. Judging by the tall grass and dried ruts, it hadn't been used in some time.

My Tacoma was a tough old girl and her 4x4 had seen me out of many a Mississippi mud pit, but climbing those mountainous ATV trails really put her to the test, and there were a few moments where I thought I was gonna get stuck, and once where I almost drove off a bluff.

I let the litany of NO TRESPASSING signs and purple spray-painted trees guide me and poor Scoot as we were thrown about. I did my best not to get us both killed as we punched through walls of weeds and tall grass, knowing damn well this whole area was gumbo with sink holes.

Eventually we came to a high point, what the topographical map in my glovebox said was "Goat Mountain," and got out. From here I could see the endless expanse of rolling green as the hills swept toward the horizon in verdant waves, and I had to take a moment to stop and gander, as one does on a mountain top. Then I turned my gaze inward, steeling myself for the horrors to come.

Dense stands of short pine and white oak engulfed the hillside, with the occasional bare patch where huge pink boulders, worn smooth by billions of years, cropped up. I loaded up my backpack and took the pistol out from under my seat and took that along too.

No, I wasn't about to go shooting demonic blights, but methheads were thick as fleas up here. Finally, I took out the Milk-Bones. I had Scoot's full attention.

I broke one in half and let him get a taste. Then I held out the stiff bandana under his nose. He sniffed, tail wagging, then his nose immediately went to the ground. He looked back up at me, and I nodded, giving him the other half.

## RICHARD BEAUCHAMP

"Seek, Scoot, seek!" I chirped. That was all I needed to say. That boy was off like a rocket.

Over hill and holler we went, Scoot shooting through thickets and jumping up shallow boulders like he hadn't been raised in tabletop flatlands his whole life. I had to struggle to keep up, occasionally whistling my two-toot call that meant *wait*.

But Scoot, normally an incredibly obedient dog, sallied on as if I didn't exist, and I was starting to fear losing the dog as my calves burned with the strain of going up and down each hill, which were really small mountains if you took into account the many bluffs and Precambrian rock formations that jutted out of the ground like teeth.

After about two miles of chasing the little turd around, out of breath and sweating like a pig, I almost crashed into Scoot as I ran through a thick wall of creeper-vine-choked trees and came upon a clearing that made me gawp and goggle like a newborn presented with her first shiny spoon.

Carved out of the mountainside was a bowl-shaped depression riddled with holes of varying size, making me think of those big wasp nests that set up in the corners and crannies of Daddy's outbuildings come summer.

The sun shone down high and directly, as the trees that tried to grow around this bitter stony soil had withered and died. Even the tough creeper vine, which could punch through concrete and asphalt like nothing, was conspicuously absent.

Despite the sun shining unhindered by tree cover, the shadows that clung to those stone mouths were preternaturally dark, more like ink smears than a mere absence of light, and from those obsidian voids I saw black vapor ooze.

Each of the cave mouths radiated not just a blackness, but a sort of deterring aura that scraped at my nerves like sixty-grit sandpaper. I felt the cheap gas station coffee I'd drunk on the way out here gurgle in my stomach like it was pure battery acid. A pressure started to form behind my eyes like a wicked headache was coming on.

Scoot whined pitifully by my feet. I was so taken aback by this scene of metaphysical wrongness that I didn't even notice the poor beagle sitting tail tucked and ears pricked back like the wings of a 747. I hadn't seen him like that since a passel of coyotes had come on Daddy's farm about two years ago, no doubt drawn in by the chicken coops and the smell of their feathery succor within. Ever since we got Gunther and Striker, our two guard-dog German Shepherds to patrol the perimeter, Scoot had never once looked that afraid.

Until now.

"Good boy. What a *good* boy," I said in my best, most soothing mama voice, rubbing behind his ears and patting him on the butt. Scoot just looked at me with a confused look of fear and need, and I felt my throat go sore at the sight.

I hated having to drag him into this; this poor dog had no idea why he was piss-scared and probably smelling God knows what sort of horrible aroma those things give off.

I gave him another Milk-Bone as a just reward for finding his target. But Scoot only sniffed at the treat, which was a first. Anyone who's ever owned a beagle knows they're the garbage disposal of dogs, and I'd never, ever known Scoot to ignore a treat.

I stood there for a second deliberating what to do. I couldn't just tie him off to a tree and have him wait. There was a good chance I might never come out from that subterranean hell.

"Aw, hell," I said, kneeling down to pour Scoot some water into the little foldable doggie bowl I brought with me. The water he lapped at eagerly, and I kept pouring till he stopped slurping. His muzzle sopping wet, I cupped his face and made him look at me.

"Scoot, go home. You hear me? *Go home*." I said. Home could either mean the farmstead, or the truck, which smelled like the farm, and I'd practiced this command enough to know he'd go right to the truck, even if it was miles away.

The dog needed no further encouragement; he took off with even more zest than he did with his seek command, probably wanting to be far away from this terrible place. I prayed if I didn't make it out of this maternal call-to-aid alive, someone would come across the truck sooner or later and Scoot, whose information was engraved on his collar tag, would be returned home.

Alone now, I took out the excising materials needed. The iron spike had grown ice cold to the touch; I could see frost and condensation forming on the metal. Oh yeah, this was the spot, alright.

I squinted toward the biggest of the entrances, praying I wouldn't have to endure any claustrophobic tunnelling. I put on my headlamp, silently cursed my momma for getting me into this, and headed forward into a place where light had never been.

My headlamp was the high-powered LED variety that could blind a man if they weren't careful, but it was still dimmed all the same by the fetid energy that flooded the cave like corpse rot. As soon as I stepped foot into the cavern, my headlamp's reach shortened down to five feet. A damned murky five feet.

I immediately started to hyperventilate, feeling that smothering concentration of evil enter my nose, my mouth. It was like trying to breathe through a wet dishrag.

I'd never encountered a blight so concentrated, so thick before. All the ones I'd helped excise with my momma were like watered down piss-beer compared to this thirty-year-aged single malt. *Christ, I'm not ready for this*, I thought, iron bands of fear constricting around my ribs.

Then I remembered what Mama used to tell me before every "booger-removal" as she called it.

"Now, Essy, this evil stuff is gonna do ever'thing in its power to turn you away. Make you feel like you can't breathe. Make you as jittery as a cat in a dog pound. But that's all just parlor tricks, honey. Us with the seein' blood, we can repel it. You just gotta tell yourself you're in control."

Easier said than done, but I eventually mustered my courage and forged deeper into that ink-black abyss. I can't even really tell you what the cave looked like, the blight was so thick. But I'd been under these ancient mountains plenty of times, and I could imagine the tan karst walls and textured orange stalactites hanging from the ceiling like stone fangs.

I just focused on what was straight ahead, until I got to the foul, diseased heart of this abominable leviathan. I'd know as soon as I got close. That's when the visions would begin. And with how strong this shit was, I knew I was in for a ride.

I slalomed through sinuous passages, the stone walls twisting and turning, becoming narrower. At every fork I came to, I consulted the deep, primal instincts that my mother had passed along with her seein' blood. The 'feeling' part of the seeing, you could say. I hesitated for only a second at each fork, letting that genetic compass point me onward like a dousing rod to water.

I knew I was getting closer, because through the obsidian haze in the air I began to see flashes of my mother in her dying moments. Arthritic fingers clutching her chest, as if to rip out that weak, troubled heart of hers. Words of admonishment spilled from her chapped, bleeding lips.

*You abandoned me, Esther. Abandoned me when I needed you most. What a disappointment you turned out to be. My only daughter, making me infertile so I couldn't try again with another kid. One who wouldn't up and run off. Ungrateful brat. Spoiled dyke—*

"No!" I screamed at the suffocating darkness around me. "My momma would never."

I tried to hide the fear, the grief, the frailty in my voice. "I'm coming for you, you sumbitch. You hear me!"

I tried to project confidence, trying to unnerve it like it did me. Christ, it was hard. Twice I almost collapsed to my knees and let loose with a throat-tearing sob as the images of her suffering bore through my brain like a diamond drill bit through a watermelon.

The passages became smaller, until I was forced on my hands and knees, crawling to keep from smacking my head on the stone ceiling above. I was too distracted with horror and grief from these hallucinations to feel claustrophobia.

Just when I thought things couldn't get more harrowing, the passage abruptly opened up, and one of my outstretched hands, cold and wet from pawing at the damp cave floor, found yielding flesh.

I froze. I know blood can't actually run cold, but God, mine seemed too. Trembling fingers sought out what I couldn't make myself see. Momma's once-luscious red curls, now stringy straw clumps upon a denuded scalp. My hands went to her throat, felt the delicate swell of her neck. I expected no pulse, but good lord, I felt the faintest, threadiest rhythm. A heart barely doing its job, ready to put in its two weeks ASAP.

"Muh—Mama?" I gasped, my hands going to her mouth, and yes, there was just a tickle of breath there.

"Esther—" My name sounded like it was spoken by the rustle of dead leaves in a winter wind.

I finally made myself look. It was worse than I expected, even though she was alive. Once-sky-blue eyes were dulled to cigarette ash. The skin jaundiced. Delicate veins stood out in stark contrast. Her cheeks and eyes were so sunken she looked like an Auschwitz victim. The simple smock dress she went to battle in seemed to house only a skeleton. Hell, even her damn freckles looked haggard.

"Don't you move, Mama, I'm here, Essie's here," I said, tears welling up in my eyes as I quickly took out a water bottle, trickling some into her mouth. She groaned gratefully as she drank, her Adam's

# THE APPLE AND THE TREE

apple moving up and down like a bobber with a catfish on the end. *How in the hell are you even alive, woman?* I marveled.

I was getting ready to grab a granola bar from my pack when she shook her head, grasping my wrist with her cold corpse hand.

"Don't. Finish. Finish it. Or I die anyway," she rasped, and just as she said this I felt a freezing wave of icy mist break across my back.

I whirled, and the already smothered light from my headlamp was almost non-existent now, no more than a guttering candle flame. I was here, in the eye of this storm, the heart of this wretched thing.

A righteous anger flooded me as this thing dared breathe its rotten breath on me. The sight of what it had done to my mother removed the fear and the terror and instead galvanized me into action.

"You bastard. You goddamn abomination—" I growled as I reached into my pack and took out the spirit box, which was hot to the touch, and the iron spike, which was so cold it stuck to my skin when I grabbed it. Both burned in counterpoint to the other. I winced, but let the pain flow through me, stoking the anger.

I felt a change in the room now as this thing tried to break me. My mother's false voice in my ears, trying to tell me how terrible a daughter I was. I realized then this thing had used my mother as bait, this thing had the ability to be cunning, which was new. Still, this realization only further incensed me as I stood defiantly in the face of that unlight.

I spoke in the archaic Germanic tongue that my mother's ancestors brought with them from across the sea and into the hills. *I am a defender of the light. I am here to vanquish the dark. I command you to be imprisoned.* I spoke the harsh, guttural words in a snarl as I cracked the hinge on the spirit box; the silver lining glowed with a red heat.

Corrupted wind flowed through the cave as this thing realized it was trapped and cornered. It blew against me, making my eyes water and my throat burn as it felt like a small tornado was let loose in the cavern.

I felt my pupils dilate as I looked into the heart of that blackness and found it. A faint red pulse, like an ethereal heart, flittering around the atrium of the cavern like a wild ferret. It couldn't run. It'd been rooted here for billions of years, and now its stubborn refusal to leave had trapped it.

I screamed as I lunged toward that carmine pulse, my right hand completely numb as I thrust the frozen iron spike into it. It felt like someone stuck a taser to my arm as the cleansing metal and the blight came into contact. Even as my limb spasmed, I kept it pinned as I opened the spirit box all the way and shoved it forward.

*In*, I commanded. It struggled, my mind afire with horrific images. *In*, I screamed in that ancient tongue. *In. In. IN—*

With a sound like a jet breaking the sound barrier, there was a brief red flash as the energy was forcibly corralled into the spirit box. I slammed the lid shut just as I felt the world spin, and I collapsed atop it.

When I came too, the first thing I saw was my mother. The fifteen years I'd gone without seeing her had still done their damage, but she looked miles better than the reanimated corpse I'd first encountered.

"Mama?" I said stupidly as I squinted against the headlamp's glare. It shone bright and true now.

"You did it, girl. My sweet Essie. I knew I raised you right," she said, her voice no longer a death rasp, pride filling it out.

We had our Lifetime movie moment, tears and desperate hugging, then she helped me to my feet.

"Get me the hell out of here," I said, feeling like ten pounds of shit stuffed into a five pound bag.

Momma took my hand and led me to safety, just like the old days.

# DADDY

## ANN WUEHLER

Johnny spurted into the open cavity of the dead fox. His seed mingled with entrails and blood. He waited, the big orange pumpkin of a moon so apt for Halloween. A mist rose up from the fox innards. Small fingers pushed through the coils and loops. A head as bald as a rotted egg crowned; a cry of anger smacked Johnny's ears.

Missus Nancy had warned him. But she had old magicks, passed down generation to generation, full of such evil and power. This getting a child was said to come straight from the Devil himself, who was said to live in Bluff Dweller's Cave, but Johnny had no qualms there. No one in Noel would deal with her openly but she sure seemed rich in chickens and fat pigs.

He would not admit to begging her advice, either. It was just local custom to deny getting help from Missus Nancy and her kin, going back to the shadows of Mr. Lincoln's war.

He squatted by the dead animal, yanked his promised child free of its weird womb. Celia would have her child.

The baby stared at him. The baby bit between Johnny's thumb and pointing finger, sucked up the blood. Red smeared the tiny, pointed teeth as the child tried again to bite him.

"Stop that. I'm your daddy now. Let's take you to meet your mama."

He bundled that snappy turtle disguised as a newborn babe in his own homemade shirt, one of Celia's better attempts. Holding it against his bare chest made him nervous as the giant blue eyes gazed up at him, as the little limbs thrashed and kicked to get free of the swaddling, to feast on him, to kill him with tiny bites, drink his blood as he screamed and screamed.

But he'd do anything for his little sweetheart.

She had wept in his arms earlier that day. *Fifty years old, where are my babies, honeylamb? I'm a good woman; don't I take care of everything? What's the matter with me, Johnny? Am I bad? Am I too much of a sinner? I don't understand.*

No doctor had ever found out why they had never kindled. He had even made a trip to Tulsa, some hundred miles away, to get himself checked but it seemed he was fine that way.

Celia had been his first and last, the love of his entire life.

He carried her birthday present to make her happy again. His back ached, his left knee seemed full of little grinding knives and he wished to slow down, not work that ten extra acres, not worry so about if his steers would sell at Carter's Auction House there in Southwest City, but he had a new life to provide for.

Fifty-two years and he could call himself a daddy.

# DADDY

The baby in his arms abruptly shredded the sturdy plaid of his workaday shirt. Claws raked across his naked chest and he let that baby fall, his fingers wet with his own blood as the baby lay there kicking before it righted itself like a strange crab, growling as it sought to kill him. Johnny saw murder in the wide, pale-blue eyes.

"You stop that, you hear? Or I'll let you starve," he shouted, more out of frustration than any real need to see harm done. "I mean it! I will lock you in a cage and hang you from the porch."

The weird baby stopped, bald head tilting as it sat on its haunches. No baby fresh born could do such a thing. Missus Nancy had warned him the baby might not be 'normal.'

Johnny waited but it just hunkered there, lips rippling as if it cussed him out but took him at his word. He carefully wrapped it again in that torn shirt, noting the long black claws retracted into the fingertips, just like a cat would have. My, did Celia not like cats. They made her sneeze and itch. How funny to bring her a cat baby.

The walk back to the little farmhouse made him tremble and ache. The child seemed to grow heavier and his arms began to spasm, for he held it away from his body, like one might hold a beheaded chicken with the blood still spraying from the neck, the eyes in the little disconnected head still blinking, the yellow beak still opening and closing.

The child kept turning its head, rather too far, to look at him, teeth bared, before it looked forward

again, veins pulsing on that eggshell-like head.

Johnny tried to smile but his lips would not obey his brain.

Rusty, the mutt bought from a traveling peddler of brushes, crouched down and went into his den beneath the porch.

Halloween had started as a mild day, not too cold yet, but clouds gathered to the east, promising some wind or even some rain. The house seemed sunk down a bit, as if loaded with bricks and carcasses that needed seeing to. Why he thought that he could not tell. The house seemed full of death.

He remained on the porch, which Jimmy Siddoway had built some twenty years ago. A simple railing, the pine boards stained a tobacco brown, the pots of flowers Celia had set out, now turned crisp and brown as winter approached.

The baby gave a giggle.

It was the giggle of a meatpacker bringing the sledgehammer down again on the head of a steer not yet dead. A giggle that delighted in pain and hurt and suffering. The giggle of a baby born on Halloween of a dead fox and his leavings.

"Celia?"

He went through the open door of his own home, his piss nearly running down his leg, his heart thumping like a fancy drum. Johnny heard Rusty's furious, scared growling as he wandered to the kitchen, where the morning dishes waited to be washed by her worn, red hands.

The living room had her stack of Hollywood magazines. She loved to read about Clark Gable, Gary Cooper, and Leslie Howard. Her crochet hook yet rested in the ball of scarlet yarn. *I'm making you a nice Christmas vest*, she had declared last January, or had it been March? She had instead made another throw, from her leftover yarn, declaring she could not rest until her basket was tidy again.

Her violet perfume lingered here, and in their bedroom, where the bed remained unmade and the basket of dirty clothes not moved to the side of the new washing machine he had near starved himself to get her. Washing their clothes in a big metal tub made it seem they were backwards and she got so tired.

"Sweetheart?"

He went to their bedroom window, and something caught his eye, swinging from the elderly oak tree. Johnny yet held the baby and it got clutched to his chest as he made out what swung from the tree that shaded this side of the house. He set the baby on the bed, even gave it a pat as he tried to breathe, as he tried to not see what he saw.

"No oh no," he moaned, walking as if he slept down the ten stairs that separated the upstairs from the down. The baby scooted after him, slithered down the stairs on its belly, stayed just behind him as he got outside, as he turned the corner, Rusty coming out to snap at the baby, which grabbed at the red and white coon hound mix.

Rusty retreated right quick and the baby made as if to follow it but Johnny's low agonized calling for Celia changed its mind.

She had climbed on a kitchen chair, dressed in her Sunday best, a green dress with a blue collar and blue cuffs. Her butterfly pin glinted from her breast. She had done up her thin, oily hair into her church-going bun, with the seven bobby pins holding it in place. One of her black, low-heeled shoes had slipped from her bare foot, and Johnny noted that she had a blister on her ankle.

The rope had cut into her neck. Her face had begun to swell, the flies walking across her slack lips, investigating her teeth, going up her nostrils.

Johnny yanked at his wife to get her down from the branch that held her. He tried but she had chosen her rope well. He got his pocketknife out, righted that chair, cut the rope, and caught her before she fell to the overgrown grass like a sack of taters.

He kept saying her name, keening it, shoving away the baby as it tried to bite at his dead wife, at its own mother.

She had a note stuffed beneath her little church hat, the hat with the green ribbon. He unfolded it.

*I hate you*, it started, and Celia's widower could not read the rest, his tears a shield and a curtain against what she had done, what she had said in her last moments. Her wedding ring glinted from her hand.

Missus Nancy? Help?

His head snapped up.

Missus Nancy had given him the means and the knowledge to get Celia's baby out of the earth. She would know how to reverse this. Celia could not be dead, not yet. He had brought her the best birthday present; she could be happy again.

Johnny turned to the baby, after he fetched the giant wheelbarrow from the tiny barn.

"Come along. You can't stay by yourself. You know how to walk yet?"

The baby grunted, head going to the left as it tried to understand his words. The little fangs flashed at him as it tried to stand but it tumbled over and lay there crying in frustration. It needed clothes but he could not consider that now.

"Fine. You can ride in the barrow but you leave your mama alone. Hear me? I'll tie you to a wild hog; you two can duke it out. See if I don't!"

So it was that Johnny and his bride of almost thirty-seven years—he'd been fifteen to her thirteen—trundled off to see if miracles were still Missus Nancy's to command.

He ate the note, determined to never read it, never know his little sweetheart's bitter despair marching again and again through his thoughts through whatever words she had left behind. The baby snuggled against her stiffening corpse, smiling at the bumpy ride.

Missus Nancy, of the cursed Simpkins clan, looked up from scooping out the insides of a giant pumpkin, her forearms smeared with pumpkin guts. She had a face that had caved in when she lost her last tooth and a scar that ran from her left temple to under her hairy chin, a gift from the Ozarks Howler, she claimed.

Her eyes fell on what rested in the wheelbarrow and she waited for Johnny to enter her yard, her silver hair tugged back into a single braid today.

"You take that right back and bury her proper with her kin folk, Johnny Sage. I already done you a favor."

Her pale eyes flicked to the baby, back to him, back to Celia in her Sunday best and the rope yet around her swollen throat. "It's close now, All Hallows. The ha'nts is already gathering. You just let her go, you hear? You raise that child and you let your Celia go."

"I can't," he whispered, in such agony he nearly burned alive beneath the mild morning sun. "She's the only thing I ever loved."

# DADDY

Nancy walked to him, took his twisting, wet-cheeked face between her dry, rough palms. She forced his eyes to meet hers and her gaze held such pity and scorn and tenderness. "You want her back?"

"I do. We got a baby now. It's what she wanted. All those sad years, she was cutting herself, she was crying out behind the house and never thought I knew. I want her to be happy."

Nancy let him go, stepped back and back and back, her overalls stained with grease and old blood and too many duckings in the Elk river. "Whatever I pull from the earth or the veil, it won't be her."

"I don't care. I know you can do it, ain't you a white witch? Ain't you?"

Her eyes searched him, searched so hard he almost told her to forget it. This could not be Celia's end. She could not be buried with rope marks about her dear throat. The old woman sighed, nodded, snorted through her nose, her breath reeking of mint and meat.

"You leave her here, Johnny Sage. Go on back home, take your son. He's yours now. Born of a fox and tainted dirt; he's yours now. She can only come back on All Hallow's. You best have salt and iron and silver. She'll be hungry. Better hide that baby."

Johnny let out a sigh, something in him whispering it might be better to let her go, after all. That she was at peace now, though the church thought taking your own life meant you didn't go to heaven. Why that would be had always escaped him. Surely that was when God should be kindest?

But he looked at Celia's bloated face, saw the butterfly pin she had treasured so, a gift from her mother, a mother she'd never met. Her daddy had gifted her that pin on her wedding day, saying she should wear it now, her mama would have liked that.

"Salt, iron and silver."

Missus Nancy rolled her eyes and dragged Celia from that wheelbarrow, the strength yet in her lanky frame astonishing.

"You get home and you wait. Sun goes down, dark comes, she'll come visit. Go on, baby. Better name him so he knows to come when called. *Bozz bozzar, mozz mozzar, kozz kozzar.* You better name that boy. My mama called someone back, she said the words, the words supposed to be Dutch but who knows. Ain't no one but me left to say them. Got a name yet??"

"Fox. That's Celia's maiden name," Johnny said, not liking her confiding her secrets like that.

Fox allowed himself to be pushed back toward Johnny's small farm, where no Celia sat in the kitchen, smoking and reading one of her Hollywood rags as bread baked or a pie cooked.

A chicken killed and blood allowed to drain into a metal pot fed Fox, who also sucked on raw chicken meat as Johnny cleaned the house and got everything ready for Celia's return.

He took a bath. He made himself chicken and dumplings, no sense in wasting a whole chicken. He set out the piece of his Christmas vest she had finally gotten around to crocheting. He sprayed her perfume on himself and Fox sneezed. He placed a vase of dried grasses on the table, because she liked such pretty, wild touches.

The baby followed him and did not seem to need a nap. It pooped and peed like a puppy would before training it to do its business outside.

Johnny decided, as the afternoon grew long, the hours going by so slow, so slow, that the new baby needed a bath and some decent coverings.

Fox screamed at the water touching him but it was on the cold side, so Johnny ignored that. He soaped the little body though it repulsed him to touch Fox at all. The skin seemed too soft, yet rough as dead leaves. The teeth kept trying to bite him, the growling never stopping.

"I don't care, you gotta look good for your mama."

He wrapped one of his own handkerchiefs about the business end of Fox and wrapped him in the multicolored throw Celia had finished, using her odds and ends. The pale-blue eyes finally closed; the baby finally seemed ready for a rest so he placed it on the couch, not having a crib or a basket.

Maybe a drawer? Yes. He picked Fox up and put him in the kitchen drawer used for old rags, towels, and potholders. One eyelid flipped open but closed again as the baby snuggled an old bit of towel.

Night seemed reluctant to arrive, even as the sky grew dark with some storm that would probably curve around toward Pineville. He drank some coffee, calling out to Celia to come watch the storm, but no one answered him. His heart shivered but he refused to let grief win. He refused.

No children this far out, as some might try the new-fangled trick-or-treating, but he had some apples he could give out if any showed up. He should have gotten a pumpkin from Missus Nancy. Something pretty, something festive to welcome his Celia.

Witch or whatever Missus Nancy was, he'd thank her for sending his Celia back, even if for an hour or two. Some nice steaks, a basket of onions, something to show he was not a taker.

The air grew cold, winds picked up and he thought he heard voices. Leaves that had clung to the flowering dogwood flew past his nose. He could smell dust in the air but no rain.

Night at last but Johnny drifted down into simple dreams where his wife held a sweet baby boy and smiled at him with her shy, rare smile.

*Ours, Johnny. Ours.*

Glass shattered in the house.

Johnny struggled to wake but found hands holding him down, fingernails cutting into his skin through his clean shirt.

"Hello, honeylamb. Wanna do all the things I never let you do to me?" A tongue licked his ear so hard he wondered it did not just tear off. Celia? Was that Celia hurting him?

He met her wide, mad, laughing eyes and beyond her, Fox struggling to get to him through the broken glass of the vase, small face determined and grim.

She smelled of violets and road kill and chicken blood. The rope yet dug into her throat, like a choker of death. Her lips turned up, her teeth turning black as he stared at her. Her butterfly pin had been jammed into her left eye.

"Sweetheart. I got you a baby."

"Not my baby," she said, jabbing herself repeatedly with that butterfly pin until he thought his mind would just snap like a ginger cookie. "I tried to catch so many times. I went with other men; we laughed at you behind your back..."

"To hell you did," he snapped right before Fox shimmied up Celia and bit her face, small, clawed fingers trying to yank her nose and ears off.

She grabbed the baby and threw him. The wind seemed to carry him and set him down past where Johnny could see. He had forgotten to arm himself against whatever evil might be out there and Celia tried to gather him toward her body, toward the growing hole of her mouth, where a green-black ichor flowed past her darkening teeth toward the breast of her Sunday best.

"Daddy!"

Something flew at Celia, knocked her down, began to devour her, something that had grown and widened and broadened. Bright red hair covered that bald head now.

Johnny reeled back but it was Celia, it was Celia and he loved her, no matter what the dark and Halloween devils had done to her.

"Celia!" he screamed. "Run! Get out of here! I love you, love you but you git now. You git! *Bozz bozzer*!" What were the magic words? Missus Nancy had said them; his mind could not produce them at this weird moment.

The dripping bloody horror of her face regarded him, her single eye blinking and it was Celia. It was Celia.

She held out her hands to him as Fox panted and crouched to the side, eyes darting here and there, but mostly fixing on Johnny.

Johnny took her hands and they were cold. He kissed what was left of her cheek and it was cold. He heard her whisper she had not meant a

# DADDY

word in her letter, not a word, oh Johnny, let me go, let me really go, Mama's frying chicken and Daddy's telling stories, let me go.

"Then, you go, sweetheart," he said as steadily as he could, as his heart broke, as something in his very soul broke at losing what he so loved. Her cherished smile wreathed her face, her eyes filled with starlight, the shimmer of fireflies. He smelled chicken frying, he heard her daddy begin the tale about crossing paths with the Ozark Howler down in Arkansas.

His eyes closed, his heart shattered.

"Daddy?"

He held nothing in his arms but night air.

His lips tasted face cream; he smelled violets.

Celia's butterfly pin lay on the porch boards and her wedding ring rolled toward the high grass of the lawn he had not gotten around to mowing yet.

"Daddy," said Fox.

His son fetched that wedding ring and Johnny put it in his pocket.

Fox's daddy bent down, his back aching, to lift his son to his chest. Not a baby, more a very young child, a child that had come to help the only daddy he knew.

Johnny took his strange son inside, fed him the blood of another chicken and began to clean up the broken glass of the vase. How cruel to break it at all, how cruel these Halloween ha'nts and devils must be.

The house seemed full of eyes and nasty grins as he wiped his wet peepers and tried to think of a living a life without his Celia.

Little fingers took his limp hand and led him to his own bed. Fox sat in Celia's place as Johnny tried to sleep. Fox stroked his daddy's hair back even as he growled at unseen things that seemed to crowd around the bed, hover above him.

Johnny heard sly laughter and shrieks.

But no Celia joined in this tormenting and Johnny knew a peace that perhaps she would not return ever again. Perhaps God was kind after all. Perhaps even now she laughed and shivered as her father got to the good parts of his tale. Perhaps she held her mother's hand. Perhaps his Celia crocheted that Christmas vest, with endless balls of red yarn and a stack of Hollywood rags to sigh over.

He slept as his new son batted away whatever had trailed after Celia and he woke well past dawn, with her wedding ring yet in his pocket.

# THE HOLLOW BELOW

## BELLA CHACHA

The hollow didn't have a name. If it ever did, the wind must've swallowed it years ago.

    Lena Mae watched the gravel road unravel behind her in the rearview mirror like an old ribbon, then disappear altogether. One moment it was there, a thin scar through the woods, the next, just trees—dense and unblinking. As if the forest had grown back over the path, reclaiming what was once taken.

## BELLA CHACHA

She tightened her grip on the steering wheel, but the borrowed truck was already hissing to a stop in front of the cabin.

Her mother had refused to drive her. "I'll not set foot in that place again," she'd muttered, hands shaking as she stuffed Lena's duffel with sweaters and a worn quilt. "You want answers, go dig 'em up yourself."

So here she was—nineteen, orphan-hearted, and half-mad from curiosity, facing the crooked cabin her grandmother had left her like a curse.

The house leaned to one side, battered by storms, shaded by trees that hunched a little too close. Their branches curled like fingers above the sagging roof. Crickets buzzed loud enough to raise goosebumps, and the air smelled like cedar, wet stone, and something faintly scorched.

Lena stepped out of the truck and the smell hit stronger—ash and old woodsmoke. The silence was so thick, her boots sounded wrong against the porch boards.

She pushed open the door.

Inside, the dim light carved out shapes from a different century. A hand-stitched rug, a stone hearth, furniture that remembered the Great Depression. The stillness wasn't peaceful—it watched.

On a crooked mantel sat a faded photograph in a cracked wooden frame. In it, three people stood stiffly in front of the cabin. Her grandmother, young and unsmiling. A man with eyes like bottle glass. And a girl—wide-eyed, with wind-tossed curls.

Not Lena. That girl wasn't her.

She reached out to straighten the photo and noticed the rusted key on the mantel beside it. The handle was carved bone—yellowed and slick, with a tag so brittle it flaked when she touched it. *Cellar*, the label read in faded ink.

A sudden *thud* slammed her heart against her ribs. She spun around.

A blackbird had hit the window. Hard. It slid down the pane, leaving behind a wet smear, wings twitching like it had flown into something it couldn't see coming.

Lena turned back to the photograph, now somehow askew again.

She dropped her duffel by the door and went out back, boots crunching over brittle pine needles and moss.

The grave was there, just like her mother warned.

A simple mound. No flowers. No dates. Just a stone, hand-carved and worn smooth with time. Whatever name it once bore had been erased by weather and silence.

Wind stirred the trees.

"She's come back," a voice whispered through the branches. It wasn't the wind. Not exactly. It sounded like bark rubbing bark. Like something buried deep and waking slow.

Lena didn't move. Not even when the shadows around the grave seemed to lean in. Watching.

The storm broke just after midnight.

Rain hissed against the roof like it meant to erase the cabin altogether, and Lena Mae, barefoot and sleepless, padded into the front room, drawn by the crackle of something beneath the hearth. Not fire… no, that had long since gone cold. This was a softer sound. Like breath. Like pages sighing against each other.

She crouched before the hearth, her fingers trailing along the ash-caked stone until she found it—a square notch that gave slightly under pressure. She pressed harder, and the stone slid back with a gritty thunk.

Beneath was a small hollow.

Wrapped in oilcloth and bound in a faded red ribbon was a book, if you could call it that. The cover was leather, rough and hand-stitched, mottled with time and smoke. The title was burned into the flesh in uneven block letters:

**HOLLOW WORKINGS**

Lena's breath caught.

Inside, the pages were thick and yellowed, some brittle at the edges. The ink was brown; a horrible thought passed through Lena's mind that it might be blood.

Spidery handwriting danced between sketches of local herbs, moon phases, and symbols that twisted the eye if stared at too long, like they'd been carved into the air, not drawn. Some words were in phonetic spellwork, strange combinations of syllables that hummed in her chest when she whispered them aloud.

She turned to a page marked with a sprig of dried purple mint. A phrase was scrawled across the top:

*For the keeping quiet of them what knocks.*

Her stomach turned. She thought of the grave out back. The one without a name.

That night, the knocking began.

It started as a single thump beneath the floorboards, just under her bed. Then again. Rhythmic. Patient.

Lena lay frozen, the quilt tucked under her chin. The old beams creaked in protest, and the rain outside slowed, as if to make room for the sound.

Then... *scratch-scratch*... from beneath her feet.

She dared to look over the side of the bed. Nothing. But something shifted in the shadows near the hearth. That damn book, where she'd left it, had slid open to a page she hadn't yet read.

At the top:

*The Bound One must remain unnamed, untouched, unremembered.*

A cold prickle swept down her spine. Her eyes skimmed the sketch—crude, childlike—of a headless figure standing by a shallow grave, arms outstretched, roots curling from its fingers into the earth.

Another page whispered open, as if by wind.

This one was a warning:

*To speak the name is to break the veil. To remember is to raise it. To dig is to die.*

Lena slammed the book shut.

# THE HOLLOW BELOW

Her sleep came in fits. And with it, a dream.

*Her grandmother stood at the foot of her bed, face half-shadowed, lips moving but the words coming backward, as though time itself had reversed. The cabin was flooded in blue light.*

*In her dream, Lena tried to rise, but her limbs were heavy. Water seeped up from beneath the floorboards. Mawmaw leaned close, her fingers brushing Lena's cheek.*

*Her voice, when it finally came clear, was hoarse and low:*
"Put it back. Put it back, Lena-bird."

When she awoke, her hand was smeared with dirt.

Lena returned the book to the hearth at first light, but something had changed. The hearth wouldn't take it. The hollow was gone, the stone unyielding. The cabin itself seemed to bristle with resistance.

And out back, the grave had changed too. Where before there was only a carved stone with no markings, there now lay something else:

A small bouquet of wilted yarrow.

And just beneath it, a whisper, almost inaudible through the wind. *"She sees."*

Lena staggered back toward the cabin, the trees seeming to bend toward her with slow, deliberate breath.

The hollow had remembered her.

And now it would not forget.

The fireplace was cold that morning, but a trail of white ash spilled from its base, like a crooked spine, leading straight out the back door. Lena hadn't noticed it last night. She stood barefoot on the creaking floorboards, the *Hollow Workings* book tucked tight under her arm, and stared at the trail.

Outside, mist clung low to the dirt like breath held too long. The ash path slithered past the unnamed grave, still weeping black water despite a cloudless sky, and came to rest at the cellar door: rusted iron hinges and a warped wooden latch, sealed by a bone-handled lock that matched the key she'd found her first day here.

# BELLA CHACHA

She turned the key. The lock resisted, then sighed open.

The smell hit her first—wet stone, mildew, and something green but ancient, like sage burned long ago and still echoing. This was no ordinary root cellar. Its walls were ringed with carvings: sigils burned into the rock with such care they almost shimmered in the low light. Not stars. Not letters. Symbols made to keep things out. Or in.

As Lena stepped inside, her flashlight flickered, catching something in the far corner: a clay jug, squat and stained, with a child's tooth tied to it on a string of knotted red thread. Beneath it, tucked into a hollow in the earth, was a small bundle wrapped in faded muslin. Lena crouched and loosened the cloth. Hair, soft and black, spilled free, followed by curled fingernails. Human.

The flashlight guttered again. Lena backed up.

The *Hollow Workings* burned hot against her chest, as if the book had its own heartbeat. She knelt in the damp and flipped it open.

More of the phonetic script now felt readable, though she didn't understand how. Her tongue tingled as she mouthed the sounds. A warding charm. A summoning. A warning.

As the words slipped out of her mouth, the cellar seemed to hold its breath. Then the woods outside dropped into utter silence, no birdsong, no wind, just the low throb of something waking.

She slammed the book shut.

Back upstairs, her hands trembling, she tried to shake it off. The cellar. The sigils. The tooth. Her grandmother had *lived* with all this?

That night, the rain came, or so she thought. Thunder cracked. She ran to the window. But the sky was dry, stars clear and sharp. Yet the grave outside rippled like something heavy was swimming beneath it. Black water pooled around the stone, spreading in silent rivulets into the grass.

Her dream came thick and feverish.

*She stood in the cellar, the sigils glowing like fireflies. Mawmaw was there, younger, hair unbraided, eyes white as snowmelt.*

# THE HOLLOW BELOW

*"You shouldn't have opened it,"* Mawmaw said, voice moving backward, every word bending in the wrong direction. "Put it back, baby. Bury it deep. Hollow don't forget."

Lena woke with the book on her chest, open to a page she hadn't seen before. Her grandmother's handwriting, clear and sharp:
*Lena must never know whose grave it is.*
*She has the mark.*
*If she remembers, the hollow will open again.*
Lena touched her palm. The birthmark she'd hated her whole life—a crescent moon above a missing line—throbbed faintly under the skin.
From outside, the sound of digging.
And then, something knocked.
From *beneath* the floor.

The silence on the phone line stretches until Lena hears breathing—sharp, shallow, then her mother's voice, ragged and strange.
"She said you'd come back different."
The call ends.
Lena stares at the screen, heart pounding. The trees outside the window seem to lean closer. Their silhouettes twitch against the deepening dusk. Something shifts just beyond the clearing, too fast to follow.
That night, Lena walks out with a lantern in one hand and a spade in the other. The air smells wrong, like turned earth and old pennies. The grave behind the cabin pulses, the hand-carved stone dark with moisture that hasn't come from rain. The ground squelches beneath her boots, though the sky remains star-clear.
She kneels and begins to dig.

# BELLA CHACHA

The soil parts easier than it should, as if eager. About a foot down, her spade hits something solid. She pulls up a second gravestone – smaller, moss-veined, and buried flat. The engraving is faint but legible:

*Miriam Delane*—her mother's name.

But the dates are all wrong.

*Born: 1962*

*Died: 1968*

Lena drops the lantern. Flame leaps, sputters, then catches again. She stares at the stone as cold gathers in her chest like rising water.

"That's not possible," she whispers.

Unless...

Unless someone *replaced* her mother.

A sound rises from the trees. A low, humming lullaby – off-key, childlike. Lena jerks upright. A small figure flickers between the trunks. Shadow-shaped, its head too large, limbs too long, swaying with a strange rhythm like it's being rocked.

Lena bolts.

Inside the cabin, the air is freezing. The book—*Hollow Workings*—sits on the hearth like it's waiting. Lena grabs it and thrusts it into the stove. She strikes a match and watches the flames lick the leather. Nothing. Not a singe. The pages don't curl.

The spellbook doesn't burn.

Wind shrieks through the chimney, and the fire dies.

Behind her, the cellar door creaks open.

No wind. No reason. Just open.

Lena descends with shaking hands, the lantern barely keeping the dark at bay. The protective sigils on the walls glow faintly, their chalk lines vibrating. The smell of sage has turned sour, fermented.

And then she sees her.

Mawmaw.

Standing in the back of the cellar.

# THE HOLLOW BELOW

Mouth stitched shut with coarse red thread. Eyes wide. Pupils blown. Her skin is waxy, yellowed with rot, but she's not fallen. She stands. Stares. Doesn't move.

Lena nearly vomits.

Pinned to the wall beside the corpse is a torn page from the spellbook, written in her grandmother's shaky hand:

*The Bound One was our blood – a child taken to pay what Miriam's mother owed. The woods demanded balance. The forest never forgets.*
*Lena bears the mark.*
*If she remembers...*
*the Hollow will open again.*

Her knees buckle. Lena stares at the stitched mouth. "You... you knew?"

A low groan escapes Mawmaw's throat, but her lips do not part.

The cellar trembles.

Water seeps from the floorboards—black, thick like ink. The sigils begin to smudge. The protective wards dissolve.

Above, something moves through the cabin. Slow steps. Wet. Too heavy to be human.

Lena backs away. "You made me a vessel."

The corpse twitches. A single tear of black water runs down her grandmother's cheek.

Later, Lena curls in bed, the book clutched to her chest, too afraid to sleep. But the dreams come anyway.

*A child's voice counting backward.*
*A forest that breathes.*
*And a message carved into a tree, over and over again:*
Forget me. Forget me. Forget me.

When Lena wakes, her reflection in the mirror does not blink when she does.

And out back, the shadow child has begun to dig.

# BELLA CHACHA

The blood moon glows thick and low in the sky, red like a watching eye. The cabin groans with old wood and older memories. Lena kneels on the floor, candlelight flickering against the yellowed pages of *Hollow Workings*. Her hands tremble as she traces her grandmother's final entry:

*If I'm gone, she must choose. The spell must be re-bound every blood moon. Or all is unbound. The Hollow remembers.*

The instructions are detailed: dried grave-moss, moonwater steeped with a drop of her own blood, and the clay jug from the cellar placed at the threshold of the grave. She prepares everything. Each object hums, as if it remembers its last use. As if it's been waiting.

Outside, the grave bubbles again. No rain has fallen. The black water pulses. And then, quietly, splits.

A girl's pale hand breaches the soil—moss-covered, nails blackened, small teeth embedded in the flesh. The Bound One has risen.

Lena steps back, bile climbing her throat. The book drops from her hands. The grave opens wider, and the girl's head appears. Her hair is matted with roots, her eyes the color of riverstone, her mouth stitched with something too thin to be string—*vein*, maybe. Her voice is a whisper carried by the wind but spoken in Lena's own voice:

"They buried me because I knew. You do too."

Lena sees herself as a child at the cabin. A girl... *this girl*... playing with her beneath the dogwood tree. A girl her mother said was "just imaginary." A girl who vanished after a storm. Lena *did* know. She's always known.

The spellbook lies open to the last page. The binding words stare up at her.

# THE HOLLOW BELOW

She could finish it. She could push the girl back down and seal the grave again. She could be her grandmother's granddaughter to the bitter end.

Or…

She can unbind it.

The forest leans in. Trees groan. The shadows stretch longer than they should. The black water bleeds across the yard. The spellbook flutters open, pages flipping in windless air. A voice—not hers, not the girl's, but *the Hollow itself*, utters a groan of recognition.

Lena begins the spell. Her voice shakes. At the final phrase, she pauses.

"Name unspoken. Life broken. Grave kept closed…"

Her lips seal. Her heart kicks. The Bound One has crawled halfway from the earth now, hands digging into her own grave's edge like a birthing child. Her eyes—those hollow eyes, lock onto Lena's.

"If you finish, I die again," she says.

"If I don't, everything falls apart," Lena whispers.

The cellar door groans open behind her. Her grandmother's corpse stands again at the threshold, stitched mouth split into a faint smile.

Lena tears the page from the book.

She begins the *unbinding* words instead, the words written backward at the end, scrawled in blood, the ones her grandmother had half-erased with a wet thumb.

"Open the hollow. Let the bound be seen. Let memory return."

The trees cry out. The house trembles. The candles go out.

The child climbs free.

Her grandmother's corpse crumples like a puppet cut from its strings. The grave collapses into a yawning hole. The spellbook burns, finally. This time it *screams*.

The Bound One stands barefoot in the grass, moss falling from her shoulders. She touches Lena's face.

"I wasn't the debt," she says. "You were the promise."

A storm breaks, not rain, but petals, bones, feathers, ash.

# BELLA CHACHA

Lena collapses beside the open grave, breathing hard. The girl walks into the woods without turning back. The forest does not rest.

The next morning, Lena wakes beneath the dogwood tree. The grave is gone. The cellar is empty. The spellbook nothing but ash. But carved into the hearth, in a fresh, bleeding hand, is a new line:

*The Hollow forgets nothing. But it forgives those who remember.*

At dawn, there is no cabin.

Where Lena's grandmother's house once stood—fireplace, hearth, cellar and all, there is only a pit. Wide and clean as a quarry sinkhole, ringed in cinder and ash. The air buzzes with a hush too complete, as if the birds and cicadas have agreed to mourn.

Lena is barefoot, walking in circles through the hollow. Her nightgown is torn at the hem, streaked with dirt and old blood. She walks as if called, as if listening to a music deeper than sound. Her eyes are open, but there's no recognition in them, only a distant shimmering, like someone staring across time.

A stranger finds her.

A hiker passing through on the southern trail that cuts through Spook Hollow, armed with a walking stick and a bottle of filtered water. He sees her first from the ridge and thinks she's a deer, a pale one, feral and slow-moving. When he gets close enough to speak, she doesn't react. Doesn't blink.

"Miss? Are you okay?"

She answers in a whisper. But not in English.

The stranger stumbles back, gooseflesh climbing his arms. Because what she's muttering—soft, rhythmic, melodic—isn't a prayer or plea. It's a spell. And something about the way the trees lean in to listen tells him it's working.

# THE HOLLOW BELOW

Lena drops to her knees in the moss. She presses her forehead to the ground and speaks the last line of the old tongue.

Then she laughs. Or sobs. Or both.

When search parties come days later, there is no sign of the cabin. Locals insist there never was a house on that land, only bad luck, rotted earth, a stand of trees nobody dared log. The maps from the county archive show the property lines but label that patch "UNSURVEYED – HOLLOW."

But there *is* something new.

A stone, upright, gray with lichen, tucked at the edge of the clearing. It reads:

*LENA MAE*

*She remembered.*

No date. No carving hand. Just the name, and the knowing.

And sometimes, in the deepest bends of Spook Hollow, when the moon is full and the fog clings low to the treetops, two shapes can be seen.

One is a girl in white with ash-dark eyes, whispering to the trees.

The other is smaller, humming in circles, bones clicking, moss trailing from her fingers. She bears no name. But she is not bound anymore.

They say the forest listens to them both.

They say the forest *answers*.

And that's why no one builds near the hollow anymore.

Not since the day it opened.

Not since the day Lena walked into it, and stayed.

# THE SERPENT OF EDEN

## D. WINCHESTER

When Robert Mueller signed up for Hoover's nascent Bureau of Investigation in 1922, he expected to fight rum runners and bathtub distillers of all types in Chicago or perhaps even the Big Apple.

The last thing he expected was an assignment back to St. Louis, but in retrospect, he should have. The humid river town's drawl still clung faintly to his own speech, despite his best efforts to hide it, but that made sense, considering he'd grown up just across the water in St. Charles Parish.

Initially, the work was exhilarating. He let his hair grow out, adopted the guise of a rough-edged working man flush with cash, as he began mapping the city's shadowed arteries of vice. Undercover, they called it.

# D. WINCHESTER

It wasn't a job he'd even suspected the existence of before this, but it was still the best damn job he'd ever had.

Nights were spent flashing Bureau cash in smoky speakeasies, trading coded phrases, and making conversation with women who would have normally been out of his league. As time went on, he started playing the big shot, and surprisingly, they responded accordingly.

By day, his colleagues would bust down doors. Sometimes, they'd even arrest him for show, but he'd always slip free of those dragnets and move on to bigger and better things. The city was rife with hidden life after dark. Jazz didn't spill out from behind every door, but he learned where to go and which palms to grease to get in.

Every door led to a drink, a deal, and, as often as not, a dame. Sometimes, he felt like he'd have a hard time throwing his hat and not hitting some gorgeous broad or another. Robert considered himself a good Christian, but it was hard not to sin in a job like this.

Most of the gals he seduced for their contacts didn't stand out after a while, but some did. There was Clara, of course. She was a dancer with sapphire eyes who seemed to know every back-alley deal and dealer. He spent weeks nursing drinks near her stage, feeding her stories of big deals coming down the river, just to hear her gossiping about who was meeting who.

Then there was Maeve. She was a weary counter girl at a supposedly legitimate pharmacy that served as a drop point for illicit pick-me-ups. She wanted a little adventure, and he gave it to her in exchange for her near-encyclopedic knowledge of the bootlegger routes she scheduled.

He'd charmed her with feigned sympathy and genuine desire while he spent weeks patiently untangling the web of deliveries and payoffs she knew of until it was time to arrest her. He never saw her again after that.

While he started as a working man, he quickly moved on. Through a web of invented relations and phantom business associates, he just kept failing upward, climbing the rungs of the underworld. Every time the Feds would come through, busting barrels and draining beer into the gutter, they'd arrest his boss, but somehow, good ole Robby G would manage to come through unscathed and take a larger role in the St. Louis underworld.

It was a good hustle, certainly safer than the bloody streets of Chicago. He might have played the role indefinitely, a career G-Man masquerading as a fictitious Mafioso. Unfortunately, after a string of miraculous escapes from the clutches of the law, the St. Louis scene grew too hot.

Whispers began to follow him as closely as the leggy blondes he favored, and one botched hit later, Washington dispatched him to the quiet anonymity of the sticks until the heat died down.

It was the same work, only this time, it was undertaken under the alias of Robert Lewis. It was quieter than what he'd been doing, but not in a bad way. The locals called the area the Ozarks, but the maps didn't bother to call it anything at all.

The wilderness was a vast, unmapped expanse that stretched between St. Louis and Tulsa, marred only occasionally by the occasional river or dubious peak. They had so much land to spare that there were plans to turn part of it into a vast lake and use the dam to power whole new towns that didn't even exist yet. For now, though, all they had were primeval forests that stretched into an eternity of humid green, broken by mountains, swamps, and the ever-present, damnable whine of mosquitoes.

To him, it was just a different breed of trouble. Moonshiners were less organized and carried shotguns instead of Thompsons, but they had itchier trigger fingers, so it balanced out.

Robert could see, even from the very beginning, how many of the recalcitrant population were lawbreakers just waiting to be taken down. He could have carved out a respectable record of arrests in that vast expanse if his investigations hadn't begun to brush against the periphery of the Covenant of Bottomless Waters.

From the outset, something felt off. Names linked to the queer sect surfaced with disturbing regularity in reports concerning rival stills or sudden disappearances. Yet, direct questions about the Covenant met a wall of tight-lipped silence. There was a shared, fearful reticence that only fueled the disquieting whispers circulating at crossroads stores.

These weren't the tales they'd normally tell outsiders, but after a few drinks or a well-placed bribe, they opened up to him, one story at a time. They spoke of strange rites performed near sinkholes and muttered about debts settled not with coin but with farms changing hands under dubious circumstances.

Darker still were tales of the shine itself. The stuff was potent but rumored to do worse than leave you hungover. Some swore the Covenant didn't use simple spring water but drew it from an unholy source. No one would say more, and even those hints were vociferously denied if he tried to probe further.

Going by his new alias now, Robby approached cautiously, making only small deals at first. The Covenant's members were cagey and suspicious of outsiders, but when he let careful hints of his connections to the Teamsters slip and spoke of avenues by which they might move substantial product east, their interest sharpened palpably.

After that, his meetings with the clannish people advanced from drinks in decaying local establishments to attending their Sunday gatherings. Those strange services were held in a stark, windowless meeting house, miles from nowhere. Outside, the buildings were rough timber and shake. Inside wasn't any fancier, but it wasn't the decor or even the people that attracted the agent's attention.

It was the air; it hung thick, expectant, and humid, like the weather before a storm. Although it never started raining, the words of Pastor Galbraith certainly boomed like thunder during his sermons. He was a gaunt man with burning eyes who preached a warped gospel full of fire and brimstone. The man often spoke of a new flood and how the waters below would swallow the world in a final baptism.

Robert thought he might be railing against the stalled Osage River Dam project, but after he attended a couple services and took scrupulous notes, he decided there was more to it than that. Regardless, it was never

# THE SERPENT OF EDEN

elaborated on. No one asked any questions. Instead, the congregation sang familiar hymns. Sometimes, though, the melodies were paired with words in a foreign tongue that he didn't know.

Those were far from the only oddities. He also noticed strange, spiral symbols carved into the wooden pews and pulpit. At first, he brushed them off as graffiti or stylized sunbursts, but they were more than that. They were symbols that didn't match any Christian iconography he knew, and their serpentine curves unsettled him; if Robert looked at one of the spirals for long enough, he swore it started moving.

Still, despite the unease prickling his skin, he played the part of a potential convert interested more in earthly profits than heavenly rewards. Eventually, they even shared what was euphemistically referred to as the Waters of the Deep. The shine itself was part of the ritual of trust.

Until this point, he'd tasted everything Prohibition offered, from fine champagne to bathtub gin. The Covenant's brew wasn't the worst tasting, but its odd, faint reddish tint and queer aftertaste disturbed him, seeding his sleep with dread-filled paralysis and fragmented visions of crushing darkness.

Still, the more he drank, the more they confided. He endured the hangovers, the nightmares, and the lingering disquiet. He'd done worse to make a case.

All of that worked well enough, and slowly, he earned enough of their trust to lead to a first shipment bound for Chicago. It was small enough to fit into the trunk of a car and had no difficulties. The profits from that little adventure were enough for them to take the plunge on a second, larger shipment.

He planned to let this one through, too, but only so the Bureau could monitor the larger network. It was on the third one, when he knew the ins and outs of this reclusive group, that he planned to finally crack down on them.

The second big shipment was loaded under a starless sky that weighed on him. Agent Mueller was getting tired of posing as Robby

Lewis. There was something in the nights here. He felt like he was being watched and was looking forward to making this bust so he could move on to bigger and better things.

He watched the last truck rumble away. Then, exchanging a satisfied nod with Deacon Cole, he turned back to his car, when a blinding pain exploded at the base of his skull. The world tilted, then went black.

He woke to the smell of damp earth and motor oil. Robert's head throbbed, and his hands were bound tightly. He was crammed into the trunk of a car driving down a road bad enough for the ruts to rattle his teeth. Worse, he was in there a good twenty minutes before it finally stopped.

Then, rough hands hauled him out and dumped him onto muddy ground. Torchlight flickered across stern faces—Pastor Gilbraith and a dozen grim-faced followers stood in a clearing dominated by a river rushing past before disappearing into a hillside cave and vanishing underground. Beside it, there was a strange rust-colored pool that was completely dry.

"Brother Lewis," Gilbraith announced, his voice echoing slightly, "your time of testing worldly spirits is over. Tonight, you shall receive the true baptism! Rejoice, for soon you shall know what it is Eve knew, at the beginning of things!"

Robert spat into the dirt. "The name's not Lewis, it's Mueller. Special Agent Mueller, Federal Bureau of Investigation, and you're all under arrest."

"We've known you were a wolf among sheep from the very beginning," Pastor Gilbraith said with a smirk. "And if we didn't need to meet your man to ensure our goods would find fertile ground far from here, we would have long ago given you your eternal reward."

"Fertile ground?" Agent Mueller asked, fighting against panic as he took in the clearing and the other two men they brought forth from a truck, bound and gagged. "What's so special about selling shine in Baltimore?"

"It matters not where the seed is planted," the pastor answered cryptically. "So long as the soil is fertile, the work will take root and flower. You could just as easily ship the Waters of the Deep to any other hotbed of sin and vice. New York, Los Angeles, or even Chicago. In time, all will come to see the truth."

As the pastor spoke, Mueller studied the boulders that might have been megaliths or standing stones, but before he could make heads or tails of it, they shoved the first bound man into the churning river. He struggled against the men holding him, but it was useless.

"You bastard," Robert growled, struggling against the men who held him. "You call yourself a holy man, but you commit murder so callously?"

"It's not murder when it's a sacrifice in the cause of something greater," the pastor assured him. "You'll see firsthand, soon enough, but first, I want you to see the true sacrament. Behold blood that is far more potent than any papist communion wine."

For perhaps half a minute, nothing happened, and then, without any warning, a rust-red geyser launched skyward from the dried-up pool, and several men and women standing by with metal pails and buckets were doused with the foul stuff as they filled their vessels.

It was obvious that they were in a state of religious ecstasy, but to Mueller, they looked more like blood-spattered maniacs dancing in the rain. "Diabolical," Robert muttered, as he twisted his wrists impotently against his bonds, opting for bravado instead of the dread building inside of him.

"Geysers aren't much rarer than caves in these parts," Robert answered with a snort. "You could have probably found a nicer one easily enough."

"This beauty is beyond a blind man like you." Gilbraith smiled, gesturing for the second captive to be taken to the river as the geyser subsided. "There's nothing natural about the water we use to make our spirits. It comes to us as a gift from He-Who-Dwells-Below."

"Dwells below, huh?" Mueller chuckled, earning a slap. "You best tell the devil that you're going to need cleaner water if you're going to make anything better than rotgut, you hear?"

"Devil?" The preacher's smirk turned predatory. "As if we'd ever pay homage to the Father of Lies. No, this is something much older. It's not a devil, but the Serpent of Eden coiled deep in the bowels of the earth. Dangerous as its venom might be, we use it to enlighten the benighted masses, not poison them."

He must have seen the obvious skepticism on Robert's face because he added, "You already know the truth of my words. You've seen the serpent in your dreams. We all have. The more you drink, the more you will understand the truth…"

That startled Robert, but before he could reflect on the thing that lurked in the darkness of his tainted dreams, a second man's scream shattered the night only to be cut short as he, too, vanished into the river. Moments later, the geyser erupted again.

That was more concerning, but Robert ignored the implications that seemed too terrible to be coincidence. It was clearly some trick, but since it was obvious his turn was coming, he ignored the crazed mumbo jumbo and focused on buying time.

"Listen," he said, voice tight. "My associates in St. Louis… the Chouteaus, the Taylors… they know I'm here. Know who I'm dealing with. They'll come looking. They know what you ship and where it goes. They'll—"

"Profit? Fear of mere men? The Covenant has dealt with your kind before," Gilbraith crowed, echoed by amens from followers hauling buckets of the red ichor to a waiting tank. "Many are the cars and bones of gangsters that have fed the earth beneath us. Their guns did not save them, nor would they save you. As to seizing our fine shine, let them do so. It's more important that someone drinks it than that we get paid for it. You've tasted enough to know that."

Robert recoiled at the memory. He did remember, and he hated it. The dreams he'd had those nights still twisted in his subconscious, and he'd gladly vomit up that red-tinged whiskey again if he could. He didn't have the chance to do that, or to escape, because once Pastor Galbraith gave the signal, two strong men dragged him toward the river, and no matter how hard he struggled, he could not escape as they threw him in.

The icy shock stole his breath as the current seized him, pulling him down into roaring blackness. Water invaded his mouth and nose, choking him as he scraped against unseen rock, dragged deeper into the earth's gullet. The deeper he went, the more his lungs burned, and his consciousness frayed. Then, a final, jarring impact.

He washed up, sputtering, half-submerged in a shallow, frigid pool. The water was not his concern. It was the air that he'd prayed for, and foul and stagnant though it was, he breathed in huge lungfuls of the stuff as he gasped and coughed.

Robert dragged himself out of the water and onto the slick stone next to the pool. He lay there momentarily with only the sound of water and his own ragged breathing for company. Somehow, against all odds, he was alive, and he offered a silent, incoherent prayer of thanks at that before trying to move another inch.

Then he pushed himself up, groping blindly in the pitch darkness. His fingers brushed against something smooth and cold. *A rock?* No, it was too light, and curved.

"A bone," he whispered, jerking his hand back, before feeling around again.

He encountered more, enough for bile to rise in his throat. He scrambled backward then, stumbling over something large and metallic. His shin cracked against it—the hood of a car. Utterly bewildered, he felt along its shape. Then he remembered the ropes still biting into his wrists. Finding a jagged edge of rusted metal near the crumpled bumper, he began sawing frantically, silently, straining his ears against the sepulchral silence.

Then, he heard it, the sound of something wet, dragging, echoing from not far away. He wanted to believe it was the sound of one of the other men who had been cast down into the depths with him, but he knew that wasn't right. The noise wasn't the sound of a man stumbling or gasping. It was something immense slithering over stone.

Something about the sound was just *wrong*, and primal terror sent him scrambling for the car door he couldn't see. He fumbled with the handle, pulled the door open, scrambled inside, and slammed it shut, thumbing the lock down.

That click was deafening. He held his breath, listening as the slithering neared. There was a soft *thump* against the roof, then a rasping scrape, like immense scales sliding across the metal. The door beside him groaned, the metal flexing inward with terrifying pressure. Robert squeezed his eyes shut, making himself small, not daring to move or even breathe.

Finding no key, Robert couldn't start the machine, but as he fumbled, he found the headlight knob, and then he turned it. In a minor miracle, the headlights actually sprang to life. That was the good news. The bad news was that doing that was the greatest mistake of his life.

The first thing the weak beam illuminated was bones. Piles upon piles of them were scattered like obscene driftwood across the cavern floor, and as much as he wanted to believe they belonged to animals that had been unlucky enough to be caught in the undertow, the skulls grinning sightlessly here and there made that impossible.

This was the grim harvest of decades of unhinged Covenant activity. His wasn't the only vehicle entombed here, either. Half a dozen rusted hulks including a Ford, what looked like a Studebaker, and something older sat rusting amidst the charnel landscape. The place was a horror show, a gallery of decay, but before he could even truly register the scale of the subterranean vault, he saw it.

The scaled thing that was sprawled across the cavern was vast and slimy. He'd dismissed it initially as some grotesque rock formation or some trick of shadow that his panicked brain refused to parse. That was impossible after the light made it twitch, though. Then, the terrible realization slammed into him with all the force of one of these wrecks. It was no geological feature interwoven with the bone fields. It was a serpent. It was a monstrous, cyclopean reptile of impossible proportions.

*No, not a snake*, some sane part of his mind shrieked. A snake had only two eyes and one mouth connected to a singular, flowing form. This strange entity defied such simple taxonomy.

It was closer to a pile of snakes, spanning a range from tree trunks to garden hoses, and in the reflected light of the car, he could see a glittering veil of eyes looking back at him like tiny stars along with dozens of toothy mouths. Some of them were small enough that they nibbled harmlessly at the windshield, inches in front of him, while others might be large enough to swallow this car whole if they unhinged their jaws.

Robert's vision swam as he tried to picture this *thing* as nothing more than a million pythons and boa constrictors, but he knew it wasn't so. Its coils moved with a hideous unity, and all the segments flowed smoothly together. It was a blasphemous hydra born of primordial depths that was too vast for a dozen smuggling trucks, and now, recovering from the light, its hundreds of appendages moved toward him once more.

*Better to have been eaten before I saw what was eating me*, he thought, paralyzed by terror.

He was pinned there like a fly in amber until the thing's coils started to tighten as it dragged the old Plymouth toward the largest mouth. That was when it started to constrict and windows started to shatter. When that happened, spraying him with glass, Robert's sense of self-preservation surged to life once more. He looked around the vehicle and saw a pistol on the floorboards.

He reached for it, uncertain if he meant to use it on himself or the beast about to consume him, but when he picked it up, it was a moot point. The thing was empty. He started to move then, as the lights flickered and the smaller tentacles entered the interior. He crawled toward the back seat, seeking a few more seconds of safety.

The car's dying lights wavered as he scrambled frantically toward the back seat, batting away thin, probing tendrils that snaked through the shattered windows. He clawed his way into the trunk space just as the car's frame began to twist like taffy.

The tortured metal shrieked as the force popped the trunk's lid partially open. Escape beckoned, but his eyes fixed on something nestled amongst the spare tire and rusted tools: a Thompson submachine gun.

A mad hope flared within him as he snatched it up and hoped that, unlike the previous pistol, it had bullets. Robert fumbled with the safety, shifted the selector to full auto, and turned to face the thing that was so desperate to ensnare him. His heart hammering against his ribs, he sprayed lead into the questing tentacles coiling around his ankles.

Now, the headlights were off more than they were on, but he could see the tentacles stutter and flinch in the stop-motion lighting of his gunfire. The thing recoiled, but it could not escape. It was too entangled with the car.

Its smaller limbs emitted high-pitched, whistling shrieks from tiny, fanged mouths. Then, from the deeper gloom, one of the larger maws bellowed. It was a sound like the deepest notes of some infernal organ resonating through the rock. The trunk-sized coils resumed their pressure, squeezing inexorably, dragging the collapsing car toward the creature's jaws.

Robert slammed the empty drum magazine free, fingers scrabbling blindly in the trunk for another. Finding it, he jammed it home and threw himself backward out of the groaning steel coffin mere moments before it became his tomb. He landed hard on yielding piles of bone, turned, raised the weapon, and froze.

Now, drawn together, no longer diffused across the vast space, the creature's true immensity was fully revealed. It towered in the gloom, a mountain of impossible flesh. Robert's strength evaporated. His sanity, already taxed beyond endurance, frayed and began unraveling as the heavy barrel of the Thompson drooped in his grasp.

# THE SERPENT OF EDEN

*What were bullets against this?* he wondered. A thousand rounds, ten thousand—futile gestures against such primordial might.

He might have remained there, a statue carved from fear, waiting to be devoured, had two sensations not pierced his stupor. First, the car's dying headlight gave one final, flickering death rattle before plunging the cavern into absolute darkness. After that, though, when sight abandoned him, he noticed something new: the acrid scent of gasoline.

*Fire!* The thought screamed through his broken mind.

It was a primal destructive force, better than any bullet. Galvanized, he raised the gun again. He sprayed bullets wildly, not just at the wreck he'd escaped but toward the other entombed vehicles too. Then, as serpentine tendrils raced for him, he pulled his silver Zippo from his pocket with trembling fingers and flicked it open.

Noting just how pitiful its flame was, he threw it into the closest pool of what he hoped was gasoline. It arced through the air, a tiny comet, and for a heart-stopping instant when it landed, he thought he'd failed. The flame guttered, mirroring his own extinguished hope. Then, with a sudden, violent whoosh, the gasoline ignited, and a wave of ethereal blue fire raced across the floor toward the creature.

At first, it didn't burn the monstrous flesh, but the fuel spilled on its groping appendages lit and spread to the fuel pooling around the other bullet-riddled cars. That was when those fragile blue flames blossomed into roaring orange bonfires, bathing the cavern in the lurid dancing lights of hell.

Then came the sound, a single scream from a thousand mouths. They emitted a cacophony in a hundred different registers, from shrill screeches to deep guttural roars. It was a symphony of madness conducted for an audience of one. If the sight of the beast had cracked his sanity, this choir of the damned shattered it completely.

After that, Robert fled for his life. The burning fuel showed him a hundred flickering shadows. Any one of them might have been a tunnel, but most of them were nothing but dark stone or dead ends. He tried three before one continued more than a few feet, but he didn't stop. He was propelled by pure terror, in a desperate bid to escape the thrashing and the screeching that was shaking the very foundations of the world.

*I should be dead.* The phrase became a frantic, rhythmic litany in his skull. *I should be dead. I should be dead.* A flimsy mantra against the horrors he'd witnessed, but that and the heavy Thompson still clutched in his white-knuckled grip was all he had.

He quickly escaped the firelight, plunging into the suffocating darkness that enveloped the world. Somewhere, in his short-circuiting logical brain, he knew that Missouri had endless caves. He knew that even with a flashlight and all the batteries in the world, he still might never escape, and that in the dark, it was hopeless, but he didn't care.

Finding his way back to the surface wasn't Robert's goal. All he wanted was to escape, and that much, at least, he had a chance of doing. He welcomed death in any clean, empty cavern and far from this cursed place. Anywhere out of reach of the blasphemous monster he'd glimpsed through the fire was preferable to being devoured by it.

The first hours were a frantic, blind scramble. He bloodied his shins on unseen rocks, squeezed through crevices that tore at his clothes, and scaled lightless cliffs by touch alone, all while trying to escape those distant sounds. Whenever he was truly at a loss about where to go next, he'd fire a single shot from his weapon. That single flash was the only illumination he had, and he use it to burn the details of that cavern into his mind.

Each time he did so, he feared he'd reveal some new nightmare creature, but he only ever found himself alone and lost. Sometimes the dread was too much and he'd curl up beside some unseen trickle of water, listless, waiting for the end.

How long he lay there, he never knew. Only some distant, subterranean rumble, perhaps imagined, perhaps the death throes of the leviathan, would finally stir him, forcing him back to his feet, back into the endless dark.

Days bled together into an undifferentiated morass of time, marked only by the gnawing emptiness in his belly, thirst slaked with gritty water, and a bone-deep chill. He stumbled on, hands raw, navigating by the memory of touch, the subtle language of rock textures.

Hallucinations became his only companions. Clara and Maeve flickered at the edge of his perception, trying to comfort him or warn him. After a while, he couldn't tell what was a dream and what wasn't. Was the faint slithering sound behind him real this time?

He'd collapse, sobbing, convinced madness had claimed him, only for that phantom roar to echo in the deep, jolting him onward. He learned the subtle shifts in air temperature, the damp breath of larger chambers, and the suffocating stillness of dead ends. As he went, his mind receded, and survival became instinct, pure and primal.

Then, after an eternity measured in terrified heartbeats and grinding despair, he felt it. A faint, almost imperceptible current of air against his cheek, that carried with it the ghostly scent of pine needles and damp earth. Hope, fragile but fierce, surged through him. He turned toward it, crawling, stumbling, following that thread of moving air as it grew fractionally stronger, a promise of the world above.

When he finally broke through the surface, clawing his way out of a narrow fissure hidden beneath ferns into the blessed shock of daylight, he was a skeletal, ravaged creature. The Tommy gun was long gone, abandoned when the last bullet was spent. His clothes were shredded remnants; his shirt was sacrificed earlier for crude bandages against the stone's unforgiving caresses.

Fortunately, his pants remained, cinched brutally tight by the last hole in his belt. He looked less like a man than some resurrected corpse clawed free from its grave. He staggered through the deep woods, leaning on trees, each step an agony. Half naked, he doubted anyone would have stopped for him.

When he staggered to the nearest road, a farmer eventually happened by and took pity on him. He drove Robert to the local sheriff's, but they refused to listen to who he was since he looked like a vagrant junkie. Still, even though they locked him up, they let him make a phone call to the local field office before they put him in a cell.

For a federal agent, that should have been a humiliating experience, but Robert was glad for it. He'd never slept half so well in his entire life as he did when he was locked in that iron cage and he was finally safe and alone.

Robert had wandered the dark for an endless eternity, waiting for something to devour him. He found the light again only by accident, but at least in that well-lit gray room, nothing but men could get him, and that was an acceptable trade-off.

Richardson arrived the next day, his initial disbelief dissolving into shock as he recognized the haunted eyes staring back at him. He secured Mueller's release and draped his jacket over the shivering man's shoulders.

On the long drive back to Springfield, Mueller explained everything that had happened while he'd been gone, while Robert said almost nothing at all. He told him how they'd had dogs in the woods for over a week before they'd called off the search. That surprised Robert until Richardson said, "You've been gone for nearly a month, Mueller. No one thought they'd ever see you again, and certainly not like this."

Richardson tried several times to ask Robert what had happened, but the exhausted man just shook his head and said, "Let's just say there's a lot of arrests in that story, but I doubt there will be a single flashy headline."

When they arrived at the field office that afternoon, he didn't tell his boss, Stevens, immediately, either. Robert wanted to, but the Bureau dealt in facts and evidence. It wanted things that fit neatly into reports. He could tell right away that the man wasn't open-minded enough to believe half of what he'd seen, and he had no wish to be locked up in a looney bin.

So, instead of explaining, he blinked away the afterimages of that burning serpent-thing and bent the truth. He told him it was a big operation but that the details were a little blurry and that he'd need some time to write it all down after the doctors had checked him out.

Stevens gave Agent Mueller seventy-two hours, but a day at a time, that stretched into three weeks. Each attempt to write what happened threatened to unravel his fragile veneer of sanity. Sticking to the beginning was easy enough, but after he crawled out of the water and saw it… well, he crumpled up and threw away a lot of pages just trying to describe the way it slithered and the way it burned.

In the end, the official report spoke only of what could be believed. He told them about the cars and the skeletons in the labyrinthine tunnels beneath the Ozarks. Though it wasn't halfway close to true, he framed the whole thing as a depraved Satanic cult that practiced human sacrifice and unspeakable rituals, all funded by moonshine.

That was the closest he dared approach the abyss. However, even that much was made more verifiable when he could finger the breweries he'd seen in those dark woods in the lead-up to his own murder. That funded the whole deranged operation.

He'd never know if what they'd said about shipping their tainted product east was true or not. Before all this, he would have been certain it was just superstitious mumbo jumbo, but now… He simply didn't know.

The Bureau came down on them like the wrath of God after that. Agent Mueller didn't participate except to guide them to a few important landmarks in his story and stand witness at the trial months later.

Agent Mueller showed them the drowning pool and the rusted spring where the cult drew its tainted water from, but it didn't erupt once, no matter how long they stood there, increasing the agent's fear that it really might be powered by the deaths of those plunged beneath its waters. They even sent teams into the tunnels he'd emerged from, but they never found the giant cavern he'd described, and eventually, when one team never returned, they blasted the entrance shut without providing any details.

Robert told them they should seal the sink with cement, too, but they told him that the dam would take care of all that. Somehow, though, as big as the project was, that didn't seem like enough.

## D. WINCHESTER

The Lake of the Ozarks project was first started back in 1912, a decade before he became a G-Man. Thanks to all the Covenant's delays, though, it wouldn't be completed until 1931, after he was long gone. It drowned the spring, the pool, and the temple, along with every foul secret that the people who lived there might have once contained, but could dilution ever truly neutralize such ancient venom, or did it merely spread the contagion, waiting patiently in the depths?

Even after he'd moved on to the Las Vegas Bureau to handle safe, normal things like racketeering and organized crime, he couldn't help but see hints of the monstrosity that the Covenant had worshiped in the outline of that cursed body of water.

The locals called it the 'Magic Dragon' and saw fanciful shapes in its outline.

Mueller saw something else.

In those sinuous curves, hidden beneath the placid surface, he traced the submerged coils of a sleeping leviathan, an ancient horror far more real and terrible than any storybook monster. And it coiled still, cold and patient, in the lightless depths of his dreams.

# ABOUT THE AUTHORS

## RICHARD BEAUCHAMP

Richard Beauchamp has been spinning dark yarns set in his patch of the Ozark mountains since 2017. Having been published in several esteemed literary magazines and anthologies over the years (*Werewolf Short Stories* by Flame Tree Press and the *SNAFU* anthology series from Cohesion Press, to name a few), Richard has since garnered a few award nominations for his work, including being nominated for a Splatterpunk award, and his story "The Sons Of Luna" being a finalist for the 2018 Pushcart Prize for best short story.

Richard lives on the eastern extreme border of the Missouri Ozarks, and can often be found fishing, hunting, and wondering those old mountains with his wife and their dog... when he isn't populating those hollers with fictional horrors, that is.

# BELLA CHACHA

Bella Chacha is a Nigerian writer whose work explores horror, speculative fiction, and the quiet violence of folklore, memory, and place. She is particularly interested in how the supernatural intersects with cultural inheritance, belief systems, and the unseen costs of survival. Her fiction often blends psychological unease with mythic elements, drawing from both local and global traditions of dark storytelling.

Her work has appeared in *Cast of Wonders*, *Plott Hound*, *Channel*, and *Incensepunk*, among others. She is a runner-up of the Defenestrationism.net 2025 short story contest and has been nominated for the Pushcart Prize. Bella's stories tend to linger on the margins—haunted landscapes, inherited silences, and the things people bury in order to keep living.

When she is not writing, she is usually reading speculative fiction, studying the mechanics of horror, or collecting story seeds from everyday conversations and forgotten places.

# D.R. COOK

Donald Cook is a writer based in Oklahoma City with a deep interest in the stories that fall through the cracks of traditional genres. His work often explores the intersection of reality and dreams, with a particular focus on cosmic horror and social commentary. He finds himself drawn to narratives that challenge the expected and flip established tropes on their head.

A lifelong fan of the unexplained, Donald spends his time researching forgotten arcane spells and the stranger side of Americana. He believes the best stories are the ones that leave a lingering sense of unease, rooted in the idea that there is always something more beneath the surface of the mundane.

When he isn't writing, Donald is usually hunting through local bookstores or exploring the cityscapes of Oklahoma City with his wife, three kids, and grandkid. He remains a dedicated student of the "weird," always looking for the next unconventional idea to pull apart and examine.

## AMANDA DEBORD

Amanda DeBord is a horror writer and editor. She has recent stories in *Phantasmagoria* magazine and the anthologies *Bound in Blood* and *Push: An Anthology of Childbirth Horror*. When she's not working, she spends her time trail running and building spooky dioramas in the woods. She lives in St. Louis with her husband, two children, and the ghosts of several cats.

## ZARY FEKETE

Zary Fekete grew up in Hungary and currently lives in Tokyo. He has a debut novella, *Words on the Page*, out with DarkWinter Lit Press and a short story collection, *The Written Path: A Journey Through Sobriety and Scripture* out with Creative Texts. He enjoys books, podcasts, and many many many films.

## TEEL JAMES GLENN

Teel James Glenn has killed hundreds and been killed more times—on stage and screen, in forty-plus years as a stuntman. Then he decided to do something risky: become an author.

He has dozens of published books in multiple genres, and his poetry and stories have been printed in over two hundred magazines, including *Weird Tales*, *Mystery*, *Pulp Adventures*, *Mad*, Black Cat Weekly, *Cirsova*, and *Sherlock Holmes Mystery*.

He is a Shamus, Silver Falchion, and Derringer finalist and won Best Novel 2021 in the Pulp Factory Award *and* the 2012 Pulp Ark Award for Best Author.

His latest book is *A Walking Shadow*, the second in the Paradise Investigations series.
His website is: TheUrbanSwashbuckler.com.

## ZACK GRAHAM

Zack Graham became a writer because he believes in magic; storytelling was the first spell he ever learned. Born and raised in Arizona, Zack was entranced by the legends found between the deserts and the woodlands, which never really left him. Such childhood stories planted the seeds of fear and folklore in the mind of a boy who was already terrified of living. His parents kept a robust collection of King and Koontz novels in the house, which ran a constant reel of bizarro daydreams in the back of his head.

Zack went on to study English in Wyoming, where he developed a deep interest in philosophy, political criticism, and the darker stains of the human condition. His short story "The Lion and the Pilot" won both "The Sky's the Limit" Challenge and the 2023 Vocal Horror Award, and he's gone on to publish numerous books, including: *Mogollon Monsters, Ghosts of Gravsmith,* and the *Hibernator* winter horror anthology.

Zack is a sober husband and father, still leaving his mark on the badlands of central Arizona. He works as an instructor for a small, rural school, where he continues to pass on old legends to new generations.

## XAVIER POE KANE

Xavier Poe Kane is still not a best-selling author, but he's working on it—one weird story at a time. A former door gunner on the International Space Station, Xavier traded making the galaxy safe for democracy for making readers delightfully uncomfortable. He holds an MFA in Popular Fiction Writing & Publishing from Emerson College, courtesy of the GI Bill, proving that even space veterans need proper training to craft nightmares.

His debut novel, *A Mother's Torment*, was a Killer Nashville Silver

Falchion Finalist, while his short story collection, *Broken Hearts & Other Horrors*, earned a coveted "GET IT" accolade from Kirkus Reviews. His darkly imaginative tales have also found a home on the *Chilling Tales for Dark Nights* podcast, where he's a regular contributor keeping listeners awake long past their bedtimes.

When he's not conjuring horror for adults, Xavier writes children's books under the pen name Poe Kane. His debut picture book, *Leo and the Spooky Forest*, also received a "GET IT" from Kirkus Reviews, proving he can terrify audiences of all ages (gently, of course, for the little ones). He's currently working on two more children's titles: *Leo and the Squatch* and *Howlie*.

Xavier lives in the woods with his wife, Morticia, where they cultivate a state of mutual weirdness alongside their three-legged dog, Jabba the Hutt. When not writing, he can be found doing whatever mysterious things horror authors do in the forest—none of which you should ask about.

(It should be noted that "Xavier Poe Kane" is a pen name, a fictitious persona, and therefore not all details of his biography are guaranteed to be completely true.)

## ANDREW KURTZ

Andrew Kurtz's fascination with horror began in childhood, when shadows on bedroom walls and creaking floorboards sparked an imagination that would eventually lead him to the darker corners of fiction. Those early encounters with fear, whether through dog-eared paperbacks discovered in library stacks or late-night creature features flickering on television screens, planted the seeds for a lifelong obsession with the macabre.

As a writer, Kurtz has carved out his niche in the horror genre, contributing stories that explore the unsettling spaces between the mundane and the monstrous. His work has found a home in multiple anthologies alongside other voices in contemporary horror fiction. These publications have allowed him to reach readers who share his appetite for narratives that disturb, provoke, and linger in the mind long after the final page is turned.

Kurtz's approach to horror writing draws from that childhood wellspring of dread and wonder, transforming youthful fears into carefully crafted narratives that examine what frightens us and why. His stories often delve into psychological tension and atmospheric dread, building suspense through vivid detail and an understanding of how the ordinary can become extraordinary when viewed through a sinister lens.

Through his contributions to the horror anthology market, Kurtz has established himself as a dedicated voice in the genre's independent publishing scene. Black Hare Press and Wicked Shadow Press, both known for showcasing emerging and established horror talent, have provided platforms for his work to reach an audience hungry for fresh takes on timeless terrors.

Whether exploring supernatural phenomena, psychological breakdown, or the monsters that wear human faces, Andrew Kurtz continues to pursue the craft that first captivated him as a child, the art of telling stories that make readers check the locks on their doors and leave the lights burning just a little longer.

## TROY SEATE

Troy stands on the side of the literary highway and thumbs down whatever genre comes roaring by. His storytelling runs the gamut from Horror Novel Review's Best Short Fiction to the *Chicken Soup for the Soul* series. His memoirs and essays report fact, while his fiction incorporates fantasy, suspense, or humor featuring the quirkiest of characters. His latest short-story collection, *Gallery of Souls*, is now available on Amazon.

## FENDY S. TULODO

Fendy S. Tulodo writes and makes music from Malang, Indonesia. His stories often circle around how time feels different for each person, how memory stretches or sticks, and how bonds survive even after someone's gone or far away. He pays attention to stillness, to tiny cracks in routine, especially the kind that hint at something uneasy underneath.

By daylight, he sells motorcycles. The job keeps him grounded in real talk, real streets, real things. At night, he records under the name Nep Kid, crafting sparse, moody tracks that live in the same quiet ache as his prose. His writing has shown up in a few literary spots, usually drifting toward the strange or uncanny, but always holding onto something human.

Whether through sound or sentences, he works in the gap between what's said out loud and what stays buried inside. He's not after neat answers. He's drawn to the unease of uncertainty, to those seconds when the world tilts, just barely, and nothing feels quite solid anymore.

## D. WINCHESTER

A veteran of the nuclear submarine force, David has lived in thirteen states across the country. He even spent a couple of years living in a van as he traveled all the way to Alaska and back.

Now, he is an aspiring writer living in Bavaria with his wife. He has a dozen short stories in print, a few books and audiobooks on Amazon, and a couple of ongoing web novels. For more about him or his works, check out his website, Caffeineforge.com.

## ANN WUEHLER

Ann Wuehler is a writer from Eastern Oregon with a yen for road trips, a weird obsession with rocks, and a cat named Jaws.

She has written seven novels—*Aftermath: Boise, Idaho*, *Remarkable Women of Brokenheart Lane*, *The House on Clark Boulevard*, *Oregon Gothic*, *The Adventures of Grumpy Odin and Sexy Jesus*, *Owyhee Days*, and *Malheur Baby*. She has also had short stories published in several anthologies and periodicals.

# ABOUT THE EDITOR

Heather Daughrity is the author of *Knock Knock*, *Tales My Grandmother Told Me*, *Echoes of the Dead*, and the upcoming *The Haunted Hours*. She writes emotional, psychological, supernatural horror, inspired by the Victorian Gothic writers she grew up reading.

She is also the curating editor of the HoH anthology series, including *House of Haunts*, *Hospital of Haunts*, *Hotel of Haunts*, and the upcoming *Highway of Haunts*, as well as the editor of *Spook Hollow: Tales of Ozark Horror, Volumes One and Two*.

Heather lives in Oklahoma with her husband, fellow author Joshua Loyd Fox. Together they operate Watertower Hill Publishing, publishing quality books across multiple genres.

Heather enjoys reading, writing, hiking, baking, and gardening. She is a lover of books, forests, old houses, and everyday magic.

www.ingramcontent.com/pod-product-compliance
Lightning Source LLC
LaVergne TN
LVHW040140080526
838202LV00042B/2971